Enjoy all of these American Girl Mysteries™:

THE SILENT STRANGER
A *Kaya* Mystery by Janet Shaw

THE CURSE OF RAVENSCOURT
A *Samantha* Mystery by Sarah Masters Buckey

DANGER AT THE ZOO
A *Kit* Mystery by Kathleen Ernst

A SPY ON THE HOME FRONT
A *Molly* Mystery by Alison Hart

— A *Molly* MYSTERY —

A SPY ON THE
HOME FRONT

by Alison Hart

American Girl

Published by Pleasant Company Publications
Copyright © 2005 by American Girl, LLC
All rights reserved. No part of this book may be used or
reproduced in any manner whatsoever without written permission
except in the case of brief quotations embodied in critical articles
and reviews. For information, address: Book Editor,
Pleasant Company Publications, 8400 Fairway Place,
P.O. Box 620998, Middleton, WI 53562.

Visit our Web site at **americangirl.com**.

Printed in China.
05 06 07 08 09 10 LEO 12 11 10 9 8 7 6 5 4 3 2 1

American Girl®, American Girl Mysteries™,
Molly®, and Molly McIntire®
are trademarks of American Girl, LLC.

PICTURE CREDITS
The following individuals and organizations have generously given
permission to reprint illustrations contained in "Looking Back":
pp. 154–155—Norman Rockwell poster, Minnesota Historical Society;
pilot, courtesy of the Texas Woman's University Woman's Collection;
pp. 156–157—girl at radio, Library of Congress; *Milwaukee Journal* clipping,
© 1999 Journal Sentinel, Inc., reproduced with permission, photo by UM;
FBI poster, Minnesota Historical Society; pp. 158–159—Japanese Americans,
Corbis; notice to aliens, Bettmann/Corbis; internment camp, National
Archives; pp.160–161—Hitler, Bettmann/Corbis; Silver Shirts, Robert D. King,
Family Fotos On-Line; P-51 fighter plane, © Lowell Georgia/Corbis;
Ruth Dailey Helm in cockpit, courtesy of the Texas Woman's University
Woman's Collection; pp. 162–163—four pilots, courtesy United States Air Force;
plane towing target, courtesy of the Texas Woman's University Woman's
Collection; U.S. Air Force graduates, Bettmann/Corbis;
back cover tear-off, plane in flight, Getty Images.

Illustrations by Jean-Paul Tibbles

Cataloging-in-Publication Data
available from the Library of Congress.

To my father,
Karl Leonhardt,
and his family

TABLE OF CONTENTS

1
A Dark Cloud

"Bombs away!" Molly McIntire sprang into the air. Wrapping her arms around her legs, she cannonballed into the pond. Spray splashed high. When she swam to the surface, her friend Anna Schulz clapped and whistled.

"Four feet!" Anna called from the dock that jutted into the pond. Anna was ten, exactly Molly's age. She wore a striped bathing suit. Her blond hair stuck up in wet tufts. "Your splash went four feet in the air, Molly! You beat last summer's record!"

It was August 1944, and Molly was visiting her Grammy and Granpa Culver's farm for two weeks. Anna lived with her family on the farm next door to the Culvers, and Molly counted Anna as her best summertime friend.

Usually Molly's whole family visited the farm. But World War Two was still raging, and everyone was too busy for a vacation. Her mother worked for the Red Cross. Her sister Jill volunteered at the Veterans' Hospital. Her older brother Ricky mowed lawns. Her little brother Brad was at camp. And her dad, the farthest away of all, was an American soldier doctoring the wounded in England.

Molly's Aunt Eleanor was also busy. Usually Aunt Eleanor lived at the farm with her parents, but earlier in the summer, she had trained to be a WASP—a Women's Airforce Service Pilot. Stationed in Delaware, she was ferrying warplanes across the United States, so Molly was helping out her grandparents until school started.

Now it was evening, and supper and chores were done. Molly and Anna had met at the swimming hole, located between the Schulz and Culver farms.

"Your turn, Anna!" Molly said as she treaded water by the dock.

2

"I'm going to make my splash go five feet high," Anna boasted. "Then *I'll* beat last summer's record, too." Arms pumping, she ran down the dock. A determined frown creased her face.

Molly watched in awe as Anna leaped into the air and did a perfect cannonball.

When her friend popped up a few feet away, Molly cheered.

"Hey, you're scaring all the fish away!" someone hollered.

Molly and Anna whipped around. Max, Anna's seventeen-year-old brother, was in a rowboat, fishing. The girls had been having so much fun, they'd forgotten about Max. The girls weren't allowed to swim unless a grownup, or *Max*, was along.

"Besides, those cannonballs were dippy," Max added. "Watch an *expert*." Setting down his fishing pole, he climbed onto the seat of the boat. The boat wobbled in the water, but before it could tip, Max pushed off into the air.

He hit the surface with a smack. *Sploosh!*

Water erupted like a geyser. When he bobbed to the surface, Anna called, "Show-off!"

"Smarty-pants!" Molly added.

Growling playfully, Max lunged at the girls. They screamed and dog-paddled wildly for shallow water. When Molly looked up, giggling and gasping for breath, she saw Mrs. Schulz standing on the dock. Anna's mother wore a sundress. Her hands were on her hips and she was laughing.

"Time to get out, *Kinder*," she said. "You, too, Max."

Molly knew that *Kinder* meant "children." Mr. and Mrs. Schulz were from Germany. They spoke with German accents and sprinkled their English with German words. Since Molly had played with Anna every summer vacation that she could remember, she'd picked up some German words, too.

"The sun's going down," Mrs. Schulz continued. "And I have fresh-baked cookies and milk in the kitchen."

"Yum!" Molly said as she waded onto shore.

Mrs. Schulz made the *best* cookies. Except for *Grammy's* cookies, of course.

The girls' towels and sandals were heaped at the end of the dock. Molly picked up her towel and dried her face. Then she put on her glasses, which she'd tucked under her sandal strap. Even though it was a muggy evening, goosebumps prickled her wet arms.

"Did you make molasses cookies?" Anna asked as Mrs. Schulz wrapped a towel around her daughter's shoulders.

Nodding, Mrs. Schulz rubbed Anna all over. In the middle of the pond, Max was hauling himself back into the rowboat. "Did you catch any fish for tomorrow's supper, *mein Sohn?*" she called to Max.

"The fish aren't biting," Max called back to his mother. "Their bellies are too full of mosquitoes and gnats."

"Well, then, come join us for cookies as soon as the boat is tied up for the night," Mrs. Schulz said. Arm around Anna's shoulders, she led the girls up the path.

Molly walked barefoot, her sandals swinging from one hand. Water dripped from the tips of her long braids. She had many happy memories of summertime swimming. But tonight with Anna and Max had been one of the best.

Molly sighed, reminding herself that her first week with her grandparents was already over. In addition to swimming every day, she and Anna had built a hay fort in the barn loft, hooked up a tire swing, and biked into town for ice cream. Now there was only one more week to go. She hoped the last seven days would be just as fun.

The path wound through the weeds to the Schulzes' barn. As the girls walked past the barn to the house, chickens scooted around their legs. Molly heard Mr. Schulz's car rumbling toward them down the bumpy dirt drive. Anna's father was a farmer, but he also worked evenings at a garage in the nearby town of Weston, Illinois. With the country at war and so many men overseas fighting, everyone pitched in to keep local businesses going.

Max worked, too, at the Weston airfield. Last summer, Molly had visited the airfield with Aunt Eleanor. Eleanor had even taken her up in a plane! Max filled plane tires with air and pumped fuel, but he bragged that one day he would be an Army pilot, too.

"Good evening, *mein Tochter und mein Frau,*" Mr. Schulz greeted his family when he climbed from the car. "And hello to you, too, Molly." He wore grease-stained overalls, and his face was weary, but he smiled at the girls and gave his wife a kiss.

"I stopped and got the mail," he said. "There's a letter from the Kruegers."

"Wonderful!" Mrs. Schulz beamed. "I haven't heard from Ruth Krueger in weeks. I was beginning to get worried."

"Who are the Kruegers?" Molly asked Anna as they all walked up the back-porch steps.

"Mr. and Mrs. Krueger are friends of my parents," Anna replied. "They live in Detroit, and they have a five-year-old boy named Hans."

Mr. Schulz opened the screen door. "Quick, before the bugs follow us in," he said, waving the girls inside.

Stepping into the warm kitchen, Molly inhaled deeply. Her mouth watered. The room was filled with the spicy smell of freshly baked molasses cookies.

By now, her bathing suit was almost dry. Molly wrapped her towel around her waist and tucked it in so that it made a skirt. A plate of cookies and five empty glasses sat in the middle of the kitchen table. Mrs. Schulz poured fresh milk from a pitcher. Then she served her husband a heaping bowl of stew from a pot on the stove.

Minutes later, Max bustled in, his blond hair damp. He was tall and long-limbed, and he seemed to fill the whole room. When everyone was seated at the table, Mrs. Schulz carefully tore open the envelope from the Kruegers.

"Dear Heidi and family," Mrs. Schulz eagerly read. "I have sad news—"

Her voice suddenly trailed off. Molly glanced up from her cookie. Mrs. Schulz was still reading, but silently. Molly could see her eyes move across the page. As she read, her face paled.

Mr. Schulz frowned at his wife over his raised spoon. "What is wrong?"

Mrs. Schulz looked up at him. Tears swam in her eyes. "The Kruegers have been taken to an internment camp in Texas. All of them. Even little Hans."

"What?" Mr. Schulz banged his spoon down on the table, and Molly jumped in her chair. He leaned across the table and took the letter from his wife's hands. As he read it, his face flushed angrily. "This can't be!" He threw the letter on the table. Jumping up from his chair, he began to speak rapidly in German as he paced across the floor and waved his hands.

Molly stared at him in surprise. Even Max and Anna were speechless.

Then Max raised his hand, palm out. "Papa," he said. "Please speak English. Anna and I want to know what's going on with our friends, too."

Mr. and Mrs. Schulz exchanged worried looks. Then Mr. Schulz sat heavily down again. "You are right. You should hear the news."

Molly swallowed her last bite of cookie. She wasn't sure if she should be in the kitchen, listening in. But then Anna's hand found Molly's under the table and clasped it. *Anna wants me here,* Molly decided as she squeezed her friend's hand back.

"As you know," Mr. Schulz began slowly, "terrible things are happening in Germany because of Hitler and his Nazi government. That's one reason your mama and I left Germany and came to America. Now America is our home, and for many years it has been a good home. We felt welcome here. Safe."

He dropped his eyes. Reaching across the table, Mrs. Schulz put her hand over his.

"But since America went to war with Germany two years ago, things have changed," Mr. Schulz went on. "Now the government looks at *every* German with a suspicious eye. They think that German Americans must be on *Germany's* side. The government has raided some of our friends' homes and ransacked their businesses, looking for any bit of evidence that they are helping Germany win the war."

Max and Anna sat very still. Mr. Schulz looked at them gravely. "The government needs to keep America safe from spies and enemies. Of course that is important, especially during wartime. But now the government is so worried about German spies that it sometimes arrests innocent people like the Kruegers."

Anna gasped. "You mean Mr. and Mrs. Krueger and little Hans are in *jail?*" Molly felt Anna's fingers grip hers.

"An internment camp is not a jail with bars," Mrs. Schulz explained. "But it is a place that people cannot leave."

"I've heard talk of the internment camps," Max said, frowning. "I heard they have barbed wire around them. I heard the internees live in tents or huts. But I thought only Japanese

11

Americans were sent to the camps, after Japan bombed Pearl Harbor."

As Max described the internment camps, Molly felt a chill crawl up her arms. Obviously these camps were *nothing* like Camp Gowonagin, the summer camp where Molly always had so much fun.

Mr. Schulz shook his head grimly. "It is not just Japanese Americans who are being put in these camps. It seems that German Americans are also being swept into them for the sake of our country's security."

"How is putting the Kruegers into some *camp* going to help security?" Max scraped back his chair. "Mr. Krueger runs a hardware store! He's not spying on his neighbors or sending guns to Germany."

"I don't know why the government put our friends in a camp," Mr. Schulz said. He pointed to the letter. "The Kruegers don't know either."

"*We* won't have to go to one of those camps, will we, Papa?" Anna asked.

This time Molly clutched her friend's hand

tightly. She couldn't imagine Anna and her family leaving!

"Ach, mein Tochter." Mr. Schulz put his arm around Anna's shoulder. "I think we are safe here on the farm."

Anna relaxed her grip on Molly's fingers. "Good. Tonight I'll pray that Mr. and Mrs. Krueger and little Hans will soon be back at home," she said solemnly.

"We will all pray," Mrs. Schulz added.

Molly cleared her throat. "I'm really sorry to hear about your friends," she said quietly.

Mrs. Schulz smiled. "Thank you, Molly. The war has been hard on everyone. Why, your father has been in England for over a year. I know you miss him."

Molly nodded. She missed him more than she could say.

"Now, who wants another cookie?" Mrs. Schulz asked. She held out the plate as if hoping that cookies would cheer everyone up.

Molly took a cookie to be polite. Ten minutes ago, she'd been thinking that this was the best day ever. Now a dark cloud had settled over the kitchen table.

Ever since the war, there've been so many dark clouds, Molly thought gloomily as she bit into her cookie. She wished that the dark clouds could disappear and that tomorrow could bring another sunny, swimming-hole kind of day.

2
A MYSTERIOUS BLACK CAR

"I know that eating vegetables is patriotic, Grammy," Molly said to her grandmother the next morning. "But do we have to eat *all* these tonight?" She held up a bushel basket overflowing with freshly picked beans.

Molly and Grammy were in the middle of the garden behind the Culvers' farmhouse. At home in Jefferson, Molly's family had a small Victory garden. But her grandparents had a *real* garden. Rows and rows of beans, melons, tomatoes, potatoes, onions, sweet corn, and carrots stretched as far as Molly could see.

Straightening, Grammy dropped a handful of beans into the basket. Her fingers were stained green, and sweat trickled from under the brim of her straw hat.

"You know we can't waste one bean, Molly," she replied. "Think of all the poor soldiers fighting overseas who would love a heaping plateful. Whatever we don't eat tonight, I'll can for the winter."

Molly wrinkled her nose. "How about if I send my beans to Dad?" she suggested.

Grammy laughed. "That's generous of you, Molly. But these"—she held up the basket—"will go on our table. Remember, 'Eat a vegetable, help a soldier.'"

Molly groaned. Grammy sounded just like Mrs. Gilford, the McIntires' housekeeper back home. "I know, Grammy. 'Wasting food is selfish and unpatriotic.' That's what Mrs. Gilford says."

"Mrs. Gilford is wise about the home-front effort," Grammy said. "However, I think the soldiers won't mind if we eat sweet corn instead of beans tonight."

"Oh, Grammy! Do you think so?"

Grammy nodded. "There are a few ears left."

Molly licked her lips, imagining the golden

kernels dripping with butter and salt. Okay, maybe not butter, which was carefully rationed, but the corn would be delicious anyway.

"That is, if you'll help me wash and cut the beans," Grammy added as she started from the garden, carrying the basket. "I'll can them tomorrow."

Molly followed her grandmother down the row, her bare feet sinking into the soft soil. "Will I have time to visit Anna this afternoon, too? She needs cheering up."

Last night, after Anna and Max had walked her home, Molly had told Grammy all about the letter from the Kruegers. Grammy had listened intently but hadn't said much more than "Umm-hmm" and "Is that so?" Then she'd told Molly to wash up for bed.

"Yesterday Anna and I found an old trash pile hidden in the weeds behind the Schulzes' barn," Molly went on. "We want to collect cans for Weston's scrap-metal drive."

"Of course you can go play with Anna," Grammy said.

"Grammy, why do you think Anna's friends had to go to that camp?"

Grammy shook her head. "I don't know, Molly. I'd heard of a Japanese American family that was sent to an internment camp after Japan bombed Pearl Harbor. But last night was the first I'd heard about German Americans being put in camps. It took me by surprise. Even your grandfather was surprised when I told him later. But things happen in wartime that wouldn't happen in peacetime."

"Yeah, like Dad being sent to England, and Mom having to work at the Red Cross..."

"And your Aunt Eleanor flying warplanes," Grammy added. Placing a green-tinted finger under Molly's chin, she tilted up her grand-daughter's face. "But stop being a Gloomy Gus. This is your summer vacation. Let the grownups worry about the war. You and Anna have fun!"

★

An hour later, Molly wheeled Aunt Eleanor's old bike from the barn. She waved to Granpa, who stood in front of his pickup truck, parked under an oak tree. The hood was up and he was staring at the motor.

"Where are you off to, Miss Molly?" Granpa asked when she pushed the bike over to see what he was doing.

"Anna's. We're collecting cans for the scrap drive." Molly peered at the motor. "What's wrong with your truck?"

Granpa snorted. "Old age."

"Maybe we'll find you a new motor in the Schulzes' trash pile," Molly teased as she pedaled off with a good-bye.

The Culvers' dirt lane was filled with ruts. "To keep out trouble," Granpa always said. Molly swerved from side to side, but the bike still rattled and bounced. By the time she reached the paved road, dust coated her bare legs. She was glad she'd worn Aunt Eleanor's hand-me-down shorts and holey red Keds.

Molly stopped at the end of the lane and

glanced right and left down Route 11, the main road into town. The afternoon sun reflected off the pavement. Fortunately, her Camp Gowonagin cap shaded her eyes. Still, the sweat dripping from under her bangs made her glasses slip down her nose.

After making sure there were no cars, Molly sped down the road. She turned right into the Schulzes' winding dirt lane. Cornfields stretched away on both sides. The stalks were taller than Molly.

Picking up speed, she pedaled hard up a hill. *I'm almost as fast as Aunt Eleanor, piloting a P-19,* Molly thought gleefully. Her braids flew behind her as the bike coasted around a bend.

An instant later, she saw a car coming her way—*fast!*

Startled, Molly steered sharply to her right. The bike bounced off the lane and into the cornfield. Molly stuck down one foot to keep the bike upright.

"Hey!" she hollered. "Why don't you watch where you're going?"

As the black car barreled past, Molly glimpsed two men wearing brimmed felt hats, dark suit coats, and black ties. Then the car rounded the bend, kicking dirt and gravel into the air, and disappeared.

"Well, phooey," Molly grumbled. She righted her glasses and walked the bike back onto the lane.

Fortunately, she hadn't fallen. But why hadn't the men slowed down?

As Molly mounted the bike, she stared curiously in the direction the car had gone. *Who were those men?* she wondered. Men in Weston didn't dress like that. And why were they in such a hurry?

Anna will know, Molly decided.

When she reached the farmhouse, Mr. and Mrs. Schulz were standing on the front porch. Mrs. Schulz's face was hidden in her husband's shoulder. Mr. Schulz's arms were around his wife, comforting her. He was staring down the lane, an angry expression on his face. Molly bit her lip. She knew Mr. Schulz wasn't looking at *her* so fiercely. That meant he was watching after the men.

"Anna's in the barn," Mr. Schulz called.

"Thanks," Molly called back. Just then Mrs. Schulz lifted her head. Her eyes were red and puffy.

What's going on? Molly wondered. Was there more bad news about the Kruegers? Standing up, she pumped hard on the pedals until she reached the barn, whose huge doors were wide open.

"Anna!" Molly leaned her bike against the door frame. A handful of speckled hens pecked and scratched in the doorway. "It's me, Molly."

When there was no reply, Molly whistled like a bobwhite, the girls' signal to each other. Slowly, she walked into the shadowy barn, scattering the hens. Hay bales were stacked high on one side. On the other side was an empty corncrib. Molly bet Anna was in their fort in the hayloft.

Why wasn't she answering? Was she playing a game of hide-and-seek? Or did it have something to do with her mother crying and the strange men?

"Anna?" Molly's voice was softer this time. Pigeons cooed in the rafters. One blasted into the air, the whirring of its wings startling Molly. She tilted back her head. "Anna? Are you in the loft?"

There was no answer. Then a faint bob-white whistle drifted from overhead. Molly hurried to the wooden ladder. Hand over hand she climbed until her head poked into the loft. Molly could see the top of Anna's head peeking over the walls of their fort, which was made of hay bales stacked two deep.

"Why didn't you answer me?" Molly asked as she clambered onto the wooden floor. She walked to the fort, stooping so she wouldn't bump her head on the rafters. Anna was huddled on the quilt they'd spread over a pile of straw in the middle of their fort. She wore a red-checked sleeveless shirt and baggy shorts. Her blond hair stuck out in stubby pigtails.

When Molly crawled through the gap in the bales, she saw that Anna's cheeks were tear-streaked. Anna had been crying, too.

"What's wrong?" Molly asked as she sat down beside her friend.

"Nothing." Quickly, Anna wiped her tears with the back of her hand.

"Then why are you crying?"

"I'm not crying."

"Your mother was crying," Molly said softly.

"No, she wasn't," Anna retorted. With a frown, she turned away.

Molly's eyes widened. Why was Anna so upset? And *why* was she trying to pretend that nothing was wrong? "She was too crying. And your father looked mad. Did you get more bad news about your friends the Kruegers?"

Anna shook her head no.

Molly tried a different tack. "Then who were the men in the car?"

Anna's shoulders stiffened. "Nobody."

"Well, those 'nobodies' ran me off your lane," Molly went on.

Anna shrugged as if she didn't care.

Molly bit her lip. She'd never seen her friend act this way before. Anna was acting like Emily Bennett, an English girl who'd stayed with the McIntires. Emily's parents had sent her to America to keep her safe. When Emily first arrived, Molly had tried to be friends. But it was as if Emily had built a stone wall around her feelings.

Not sure what else to say, Molly picked at a piece of straw and waited. Maybe Anna would get tired of the silent treatment and tell her what was going on.

Leaning back on the quilt, Molly stretched out her legs. Aunt Eleanor's Keds were coated with dust. Molly stuck her toe through a hole and wiggled it. "My friend Emily from England called her sneakers 'plimsolls,'" she said after a while. "Isn't that a funny word?"

Anna tried to smile, but she didn't say a word. Molly sighed. Last night they'd had so much fun swimming. And before saying good-bye, they'd made the plans to collect cans. Now for some reason, her friend wasn't up to Molly's company.

Molly sat up. "I guess I'd better go home. We'll collect cans tomorrow. Um, I hope you'll feel better soon."

Anna nodded, but she didn't look up.

Taking off her Camp Gowonagin cap, Molly set it awkwardly on Anna's head. "Gowonagin, Gowonagin. Go on again and try," Molly sang, hoping the camp cheer might *cheer* up her friend. "You can win. You can win. Go on again and try."

But Anna's shoulders stayed hunched. Molly sighed again. "See you tomorrow," she said before scooting from the fort to the ladder. Molly climbed down carefully and walked to her bike. Without her cap, she had to squint in the bright sun.

Jumping on the bike, she pedaled away from the barn and past the house. Mr. and Mrs. Schulz were no longer on the porch, and the front door was shut.

With a puzzled frown, Molly started down

the lane toward home. Anna might deny
that the two men had visited, but Molly knew
they *had*. That meant her friend was hiding
something.

Something that made Mr. Schulz angry.
Something that made Anna and her mother cry.
Did it have to do with the Kruegers' letter?

As Molly pedaled along the rutted lane,
she couldn't stop thinking about the letter, the
two men, her friend Anna, and the mysterious
goings-on at the Schulzes.

3
RUMORS

Halfway down her grandparents' lane, Molly spied a cluster of daisies growing in the weeds. She steered the bike to the side and stopped to pick a bunch. In the distance, she could see the Culvers' farmhouse and the white picket fence that framed the yard. She spotted Granpa, a speck in front of his pickup.

Molly let out a relieved sigh. There were no black cars or men in suits. Everything seemed okay at their house.

"That doesn't look like a Ford motor to me," Granpa joked when she rode up, clutching the daisies in one hand. Oil and grease from the motor striped his cheeks.

"Anna and I didn't get a chance to go through the trash pile," Molly explained.

"Um, I've got to help Grammy," she added before riding off. She didn't want to talk to Granpa about the men at the Schulzes' farm. Granpa believed in minding his own business.

She left the bike by the back porch. Grammy was in the kitchen, putting glass jars full of beans into a steaming pot on the stove. She wore a flowered housedress and a white apron. "Just in time, Molly," she said. "Since I'm busy with beans, you can pick half a dozen ears of corn for dinner."

"I will as soon as I put these daisies in water."

"My, they're pretty. And to think they grow wild. There's a vase in the bottom cupboard."

Molly set the daisies on the counter by the sink and opened the cupboard door. "Grammy, something funny is going on at the Schulzes'."

"Funny?" Grammy repeated, her attention on the steaming pot.

"Strange." Molly pulled out the vase. As she arranged the daisies, she explained all that had happened.

Grammy turned from the stove and dried her hands on her apron. "My, that does sound strange." Her brow creased with worry. "Although—"

Just then Granpa came into the kitchen, the screen door slamming behind him.

"Whew! I'm burning up," he said, mopping his brow with a handkerchief. "Must be a hundred degrees in the shade. And it's not much better in the kitchen, Mrs. Culver. Do you have to can beans in the heat of the summer?"

"If you want beans this winter, I do, Mr. Culver," Grammy said right back.

Walking over to the sink, Granpa poured himself a glass of water. Molly busied herself with the daisies. Grammy busied herself with the canning jars. As Granpa drank, he glanced from Molly to Grammy. "Did I interrupt something, ladies?"

"Molly was just telling me about the Schulzes," Grammy replied.

"What about the Schulzes?"

"Seems two strange men visited them this afternoon." Grammy caught Granpa's eye and added quietly, "You know what the town folks are saying."

Granpa lowered the glass. "Now, Mrs. Culver, that's just foolish gossip. Who would believe that a hardworking farmer like Fritz Schulz could be of interest to the FBI?"

Molly jerked back. *The FBI!* She wasn't sure what the letters stood for, but Miss Campbell, her third-grade teacher, had told the class about the FBI when they were working on the Lend-A-Hand project. She had explained that the FBI "lent a hand" by keeping America safe from spies. Afterward, Molly and her friends had pretended to look for dangerous spies, just like the FBI agents.

"Why would the FBI be watching the *Schulzes?*" Molly asked, astonished at the thought.

Grammy took a deep breath. "We don't know that they are, Molly," she said. "We've just heard *rumors*." She paused to lift several jars from the big pot, then turned back to Molly. "Some folks in town whisper that the Schulzes are being watched because they're aliens."

"Aliens?" Molly crinkled her brows. The only aliens she'd ever heard of were creatures from Mars, like the ones on the Flash Gordon radio show.

"Aliens are foreigners. Even though Max and Anna were born in the United States, you see, Mr. and Mrs. Schulz are still citizens of Germany." Grammy put an arm around Molly's shoulder. "I guess some folks wonder which side the Schulzes are on now that America is at war with Germany."

"Folks ought to mind their own business," Granpa said gruffly.

"But something *is* going on at the Schulzes', Granpa," Molly protested. "I *saw* two men in a black car driving away from the Schulzes' farm. And afterward Anna and her mother were crying."

Granpa's bushy gray brows dipped, making him look stern. "The Schulzes do not need anyone meddling in their business, Miss Molly."

"But Anna is my friend!"

"Molly." Grammy bustled over. "Why don't you take the vase of daisies into the dining room and set it on the table. The room needs brightening."

Molly stuck out her lower lip.

"Go on," Grammy urged her with a smile.

Grasping the vase with both hands, Molly reluctantly left the kitchen, her thoughts swirling. Grammy's explanation added to Mr. Schulz's explanation from last night, but Molly was still puzzled how anyone could think the Schulzes had suddenly turned into German spies. She walked slowly down the hall, knowing Granpa would say more. Granpa was famous for having the last word.

"You shouldn't be filling Molly's head with gossip," she heard Granpa say. "Especially since the talk in town is getting worse. Yesterday Henry at the gas station said that Max shouldn't be working at the airfield. 'No German should be working on American planes!' That's what Henry said. And Estelle at the diner—"

"Now, Frank, you're right. We *shouldn't* be filling Molly's head with gossip," Grammy interrupted, her usually gentle voice steely. "So let's put an end to this kind of talk. We need to let Molly know we support the Schulzes. Why, Max and his family are as loyal to America as we are."

"I'm just repeating what I heard," Granpa stated. Then Molly heard the plunk of the glass and the slam of the screen door.

Molly hurried down the hall into the dining room. Granpa may have gotten in the last word, but as far as Molly was concerned, Grammy had gotten in the most important ones: *Max and his family are as loyal to America as we are.*

The FBI had just gotten things mixed up.

★

Whooo–ooo, the train whistle rang out from her grandparents' radio that evening. Molly lay on the oval rag rug in the living room, her chin propped on her palms. Then a deep voice announced, "Central Broadcasting Systems presents: *I Love a Mystery!*"

It was dusk. Grammy was upstairs. Granpa was in the barn, checking on a cow about to calve. The front door was open to the porch. Through the screen door, Molly could hear the singing of tree frogs. A cow lowed in the distance.

Before turning on the radio, Molly had switched off the front-porch light and the living-room lamp. She wanted it dark and spooky for her favorite radio show, *I Love a Mystery.* In every episode, the detectives from the A-1 Detective Agency outwitted fiends, villains, and culprits.

This week, she'd been listening to an episode called "Temple of the Vampires."

The A-1 Detectives, Doc Long, Jack Packard, and Reggie York, were in a jungle temple, knee-deep in trouble. *Vampire* trouble. But tonight, Molly's attention kept straying from the radio adventure.

Were the men at the Schulzes' farm FBI agents? And if they were, did they really think Max and Mr. Schulz were German spies?

Oh, if only I were Doc or Jack, Molly thought dejectedly. *I'd have this mystery solved in a finger snap.*

Reeeeeeeeeee! Dong-dong-dong. Molly turned up the radio volume. A siren wailed and eerie music filled the room. She shivered. *It's only pretend,* she reminded herself.

Then she heard a thump over the sound of the music. And it wasn't coming from the radio.

Thump. Bump. The noise was coming from the front porch. Chills raced up Molly's arms. She knew it wasn't Grammy out there. Grammy was still upstairs. And it wasn't Granpa. He always came in through the back door.

Vampires? Aliens? FBI agents? Molly gulped. Half-frozen with fear, she forced her gaze toward the door.

A shadowy figure was silhouetted through the screen.

Someone *was* on the front porch!

"Wh-wh-who's there?" Molly croaked as the porch door creaked open.

4
CLOSING IN

The screen door flew wide. Heart pounding, Molly leaped to her feet as the shadowy figure stepped into the darkened front hall. It had a bullet-shaped head with round, bulgy eyes.

Molly's heart thudded. *An alien!*

"What's up, Doc?" the alien asked cheerily.

"Not m-much, Dutch," Molly answered automatically, surprised by the familiar greeting. She stepped closer. "Aunt Eleanor?"

"None other. Why is it so dark in here?" Suddenly, the hall light flicked on, spilling light across the room. It *was* Aunt Eleanor.

Relieved, Molly ran into her arms. "I'm so glad it's you!"

"Well, me too." Aunt Eleanor returned her hug, then held Molly at arm's length. "Who were you expecting? You look like you've seen a ghost."

Molly giggled. "I was listening to *I Love a Mystery* on the radio. This episode is called 'Temple of the Vampires' and, well, when I heard you at the door, I thought... Oh, never mind. I'm just glad it's you!"

Molly stepped back and looked at her aunt. She wore her leather pilot's helmet and tan one-piece coveralls that the WASPs called a "zoot suit." Her goggles were perched on top of her head.

Molly turned the radio volume down. "No one told me you were coming home," she said. "Your helmet and goggles made you look like an alien."

"Sorry about that." Aunt Eleanor pulled off her helmet, and her brown curls bounced free. "I kept them on because Max gave me a ride home from the airfield on his motor scooter."

Just then, Max pushed the screen door open and stepped inside. He held a brown leather suitcase in one hand, a duffel bag in the other. "Where would you like these?" he asked Eleanor.

"Just set them on the hall floor."

Max gave Molly a friendly smile. She looked at her bare feet, suddenly tongue-tied. All she could think about was the men at the Schulzes' farm. Did Max know about them? Did he know who they were?

And did he know what folks in Weston were saying about him?

"Thanks again for the ride, Max," Eleanor said as she escorted him outside. "I'll see you in the morning at the airfield."

"Bye, Max," Molly called, hoping she hadn't seemed rude. "Say hi to Anna for me."

"Where are Mom and Dad?" Aunt Eleanor asked when he'd left.

Just then footsteps clattered on the wooden stairs. "Eleanor! Is that you?" Grammy exclaimed as she hurried downstairs. "What a nice surprise! Oh, sweetheart, I'm so glad to see you."

Grammy and her daughter hugged. "What are you doing here?" Grammy asked.

"I'm ferrying a P-51 to Texas," Eleanor explained. "Since Weston is on the flying route, I got permission to land at the airfield for the night."

"Just for tonight?" Molly asked, trying to keep the disappointment from her voice.

Aunt Eleanor tugged gently on Molly's braid. "Just for tonight. But I couldn't fly over Illinois without stopping to see my favorite niece."

"Did you have supper?" Grammy bustled around the living room, turning off the radio and switching on a second lamp. "How about some peach cake and lemonade? Molly, grab your aunt's duffel bag, please, and put it in her bedroom."

Molly raced up the steps, carrying the duffel bag. Suddenly, her earlier scare seemed silly. *Aliens. FBI agents. Vampires.* What was she thinking? Those things only happened on radio shows.

"Now tell us about this P-51," Grammy was saying as Molly came back downstairs. Molly hurried into the kitchen, eager to hear about Eleanor's plane. She had seen photos of the new plane in the Jefferson newspaper, but she'd never seen a real one.

Granpa and Eleanor were sitting at the table with glasses of lemonade. Grammy was at the counter slicing the peach cake. Molly slid into an empty chair. Usually seconds for dessert were unheard-of. Sugar and butter were too scarce. But Aunt Eleanor's surprise visit called for something special.

Molly crossed her fingers, hoping she'd get some time with her aunt—even if it was just a few minutes to check the night sky for shooting stars, as they'd done every summer before.

"The P-51 Mustang is a new fighter plane," Eleanor said, her blue eyes flashing. "What a dream to fly!"

While Molly listened, she slowly ate her peach cake, savoring every bite. The last time Molly had visited the farm, Aunt Eleanor had taken her flying. Now, as Eleanor talked about the P-51, Molly could feel the wind rushing past as the plane dipped and soared.

"It's compact, only thirty-two feet long, but what a sleek, powerful machine," Aunt Eleanor went on. "Sweet, smooth, and fast."

Granpa chuckled. "Sounds like you're talking about a racehorse."

"It was named after the mustang, a horse the Indians liked to ride. But my speedy animal will pursue German fighter planes." Aunt Eleanor's voice rose excitedly. "It's designed to protect our bombers—to go in pursuit of the German Fw 190's and Me 262's and send them crashing."

"Wow," Molly breathed. "I wish *I* could fly a P-51 and shoot down—"

"I believe that's enough war talk." Molly suddenly felt Grammy's hand on her shoulder. "Molly, it's time for bed."

"Awww. Now? I want to hear more of Aunt Eleanor's stories."

"Yes, *now*, dear." Grammy's voice was firm. "You can read for a few minutes if you wish."

Reluctantly, Molly pushed back her chair. "Good night, Grammy. Good night, Granpa. Good night, Aunt Eleanor."

"I'll come up and tuck you in later," Aunt Eleanor whispered.

"Promise?"

"Promise."

Molly took the promise and hurried upstairs. She washed, brushed her teeth, changed into pajamas, and slid between the sheets. The small bedroom was tucked under the eaves, and it was still warm from the hot day. Molly left the door and window open, hoping for a breeze. She picked up an old book of Aunt Eleanor's, *Nancy's Mysterious Letter,* that lay on the bedside stand. She was on chapter two. Nancy Drew was trying to find a stolen mail pouch.

CLOSING IN

Molly opened the book and tried to read, but the voices coming from the kitchen kept distracting her.

She propped her head on one arm and listened. She could hear Granpa's gruff voice and Eleanor's higher one. Were they arguing? She sat up, curiosity making her too restless to read. The only cure was to find out what they were discussing.

On tiptoe, Molly sneaked to the top of the stairs.

"The child does not have to know everything," Granpa was saying in a tone that implied, *This is the last word.*

"But this concerns her friend Anna's family," Aunt Eleanor said.

Molly caught her breath. Not only was her aunt *not* letting Granpa have the last word, she was talking about the Schulzes!

Bumping down several steps, Molly peered through the banister rails. She couldn't see into the kitchen, but she could clearly hear the conversation.

"She has a right to know what's going on," Aunt Eleanor continued.

"But Eleanor, it's just town gossip," Grammy said.

"It's *not* just gossip. Mr. Kay, the manager at the airfield, told me that he's being pressured to fire Max because the Schulzes are German. How foolish!"

"Who's pressuring Mr. Kay?" Granpa asked.

Molly wedged one shoulder between the rails, trying to hear Eleanor's answer. Instead she heard the scrape of chair legs on the floor. Then her aunt said, "I've got to say good night to Molly."

Molly jerked back, banging the top of her head on the handrail. *Ouch!* Rubbing her head, she raced up the steps and into her bedroom. She launched herself onto the mattress, drew the sheet up to her chin, and opened her book.

"Reading, Molly?"

"Oh, yes—*Nancy's Mysterious Letter.*"

Aunt Eleanor came in and sat on the edge of the bed. "It might help if the book were right-side up."

Molly's cheeks reddened, and her aunt laughed. "Come on, let's look at the night sky," she suggested. "This might be our only chance."

Hand in hand, the two went over to Molly's window. Aunt Eleanor pushed back the curtains. Together they leaned on the sill and stared out, their shoulders touching.

"Can you see the North Star?" Molly asked.

Aunt Eleanor tipped her head back. "Let's find the Little Dipper first." For a few minutes, the two scanned the sky. Then Aunt Eleanor said, "It's funny, but before I came upstairs to say good night, I thought I heard the sound of running feet. Could it be that someone was on the steps listening?"

"Oops. You caught me." Molly grinned. "You should be working for the A-1 Detective Agency." Then she sighted the Little Dipper and found the bright star at the end of it. "Look, there's the North Star."

"Yup. You found it. Too bad it doesn't shine during the day. Sometimes when I'm flying, I get lost. The North Star would help me find my way."

"If you get lost, how *do* you find your way?"

"I use the IFR system."

Molly tilted her head and stared at her aunt. "What's that?"

"Pilots joke that it means 'I followed the railroad.' Railroad tracks are easy to see from the air. And they always lead to a town. Then you locate the town on your map and find your way from there." Aunt Eleanor squeezed Molly's hand. "Are you feeling a little lost today, Molly?"

Molly nodded.

"Want to tell me what's bothering you?"

In a rush, Molly told Aunt Eleanor about the strange men she'd seen driving away from the Schulzes' house and the gossip about Anna's family. She hoped Aunt Eleanor would have reassuring answers. But her aunt only sighed.

"I wish I knew what was going on, too," she replied. "Before I leave in the morning, I'll talk to Mr. Kay at the airfield. Maybe I can discover something."

Molly squeezed her aunt's hand back. She was glad Aunt Eleanor was on her side. They'd be a team—just like Jack Packard and Doc Long—and maybe together they could help the Schulzes.

★

The next morning, Granpa steered his truck down Route 11. While he drove, he grumbled about gas rationing. "We'll run out of gas before we get to the airfield," he muttered.

Molly sat in the front seat, happily squished between her grandfather and her aunt. When they turned down the lane to the Weston airfield, Aunt Eleanor pointed toward the flat, mowed field that stretched in front of the hangar, a huge, garage-like building where the mechanics worked on planes. A row of planes sat on the grassy field, their propellers pointed in the same direction.

"There's my P-51 Mustang," Aunt Eleanor said proudly. "Isn't it a beaut?"

Molly craned her neck, trying to see through the side window. She spotted a shiny plane with a star on the side, which she recognized as the "beaut." Then she spied a lone car parked to the left of the planes. It was black and dusty and looked identical to the car that had run her off the Schulzes' lane.

"Why don't you park next to that black car, Dad," Aunt Eleanor said.

When Granpa stopped the truck, Molly jumped out after her aunt. Curious, she peered into the closed car window, half expecting to see the men in black suits.

"Come on, Molly." Aunt Eleanor waved to her, and Molly ran over to join her by the

CLOSING IN

P-51. The sun glinted off its sleek silver body. A white star in a blue circle was painted on the side. White bars jutted from the circle like rectangular wings. Granpa was walking around the plane, inspecting it.

"It *is* a beaut!" Molly exclaimed.

Aunt Eleanor laughed. "You can sit in the cockpit while I do my check-over."

"Golly, can I?" Molly instantly forgot about the black car. "How do I get up there?"

Aunt Eleanor stood beside the left wing. "Step on this wooden block and then onto the wing. I'll boost you from behind."

With her aunt's help, Molly pulled herself onto the wing. Her aunt climbed up beside her and walked a few steps down the wing to the cockpit. She slid back the glass canopy that covered the cockpit.

"Swing your right leg into the cockpit," she instructed Molly. "Step on the seat and then slide down inside. Put one leg on each side of the control stick. But watch out, the cockpit floor's a long step down."

Heart racing with excitement, Molly followed her aunt's directions until she was seated in the cockpit. Before her was the instrument panel, a maze of circular gauges. Molly had no idea what the switches, levers, and numbers meant, but it didn't matter. Her head was in the clouds!

"Here." Aunt Eleanor slid her helmet onto Molly's head and then handed her the goggles. Molly snapped on the helmet and put on the goggles. The headset was hanging on the control stick. "May I?" she asked, picking it up.

"Go ahead. But don't touch anything else. I don't want you flying off without me."

Molly put the headset over her ears. With her right hand on the control stick and her left hand on the throttle, she pretended she was flying the plane. "Rrrr. Zooom." She swayed and bounced in the seat. When she glanced out the windshield, she imagined an enemy Fw 190 flying straight for her.

Molly's fantasy evaporated as she noticed

two men striding purposefully across the field. One man was short and skinny, the other tall and bulky. Both wore black suits and felt hats with brims. Molly caught her breath, recognizing the shorter man. He'd been driving the car that ran her off the Schulzes' lane!

Molly took off the headset and goggles and knelt on the cockpit seat to get a better view. Granpa and Aunt Eleanor were chatting in front of the plane's nose.

"Enemy aircraft approaching," Molly called out to them.

The warning came too late. Pushing around Granpa, the men swooped upon Aunt Eleanor. They flanked her like guards.

"Are you Miss Eleanor Culver?" the short man asked.

"Yes, I am," Aunt Eleanor replied.

"Are you the pilot of this plane?"

"Why, yes. I'm a WASP, and I'm ferrying the plane to Texas. Would you like to see my flying orders?" Aunt Eleanor started to reach into the pocket of her zoot suit.

Ignoring her question, the tall man thrust something under her nose. "Can you explain this?" He held out a piece of sturdy yellow paper about the size of a postcard. Molly glimpsed a flash of red, white, and blue, as if the American flag was shown on one side.

Aunt Eleanor glanced at it. "What is it?"

"Just answer the question."

"Would you gentlemen mind explaining what's going on here?" Granpa asked.

Neither man acknowledged him. "Answer the question, Miss Culver," the tall man repeated.

Eleanor looked again at the yellow paper and then shook her head. "I have no idea what it is."

"Then how do you explain the fact that several stacks of these leaflets were hidden in your plane?" the tall man asked.

Aunt Eleanor frowned in confusion. "Hidden in *my* plane? I don't understand."

Grasping Eleanor's upper arm, the shorter

man led her forcefully around to the left wing. "We discovered them in the empty ammunition receptacle."

Molly peered over the side of the cockpit, watching as he rapped on top of the wing. She could see the outline of a panel about midway along the span.

"Why were you snooping in this plane?" Aunt Eleanor asked, her eyes narrowed. "It's an army warplane."

"We found these leaflets during a routine check. We're inspecting all incoming planes," the shorter man replied tersely. "The government takes airfield security very seriously."

"I understand about security," Aunt Eleanor said. "What I *don't* understand is how those leaflets got into my plane. When I landed last night, I did *my* routine check. The ammunition receptacles were empty."

"So you say." The tall man gave Eleanor an accusing look as he slid the leaflet into his pocket. "You need to come with us," he added, grasping her other arm.

"Come with you?" Granpa questioned. "Now wait just a minute. Who are you? And what right—"

The short man flipped open a black wallet with his free hand and flashed a badge. "We're FBI agents. We have the authority to handle any matter that concerns the nation's security."

Molly watched, cold with horror. The men *were* FBI agents. And they were taking Aunt Eleanor!

5
ACCUSATIONS

"Wait just a minute here," Granpa protested. "You can't take my daughter. She's not a threat to security. She's a pilot working for the United States Army!"

Without a glance at Granpa, the FBI agents hustled Aunt Eleanor across the airfield. Granpa hurried after them, still protesting.

Molly tore off the helmet and climbed from the cockpit onto the wing. She inched to the back edge and looked down. Then she closed her eyes and jumped, landing hard. By the time Molly scrambled to her feet and ran around to the front of the plane, Aunt Eleanor was in the black car. As it pulled away, Granpa ran alongside, shouting, "Where are you taking my daughter?"

The black car roared from the airfield.

"Granpa, those are the same men who were at the Schulzes' farm!" Molly exclaimed when she ran up to him.

"Are you sure?" He stared after the car. His face was pale under the brim of his hat. Molly had never seen him look so lost.

"At least the shorter man is the same. He was driving yesterday."

"Well, FBI agents or not, there'd better be an explanation why they're taking *my* daughter," Granpa declared. "Perhaps Mr. Kay knows what's going on."

Granpa squared his shoulders and marched toward the small brick terminal, set about two hundred yards to the left of the hangar. Molly hurried after him, into the main lobby and down a short hallway to a door labeled "Airport Manager." When Granpa stormed into the office without taking off his hat, Molly knew he was good and mad. Molly stopped in the doorway, afraid that Granpa would send her away if he saw her.

Startled by the interruption, Mr. Kay rose from his desk chair. He wore a bow tie and a light blue shirt with a gold-embossed emblem on the pocket that said "Arnold Kay, Manager." A navy blue suit coat was draped over the back of his chair.

"Mr. Culver! May I help you?" he asked, his brows drawn together in concern. He had a fashionably thin moustache and his gray-streaked hair was smoothed back with pomade.

"*Someone* had better," Granpa sputtered. "The FBI has taken my daughter. I want to know what's going on."

Mr. Kay shook his head slowly. "I'm so sorry. The FBI assigned agents Platt and Danvers to the airport. They've been routinely checking planes flying in and out of the airport. This morning, they found stacks of anti-American leaflets hidden in the plane your daughter is ferrying to Texas."

Suddenly, Mr. Kay's attention moved to the doorway and he nodded toward Molly.

"Are you sure you want a child hearing this?"

Granpa swung around. "Molly, you go wait by the truck. I'll be out in a minute."

Molly knew better than to argue. "Yes, sir." She took a few plodding steps down the hall. Then she turned and flattened against the wall by the office door to listen. She *had* to know what was happening to Aunt Eleanor.

"The leaflets found in Eleanor's plane were full of anti-American propaganda," Mr. Kay was telling Granpa. "The FBI has reason to believe that someone from this airport has been smuggling them. The government takes the issue of propaganda very seriously. The FBI agents have no choice but to question your daughter."

Mr. Kay's voice took on a reassuring tone. "The leaflets could have been placed in the plane by someone else. That's what I told the FBI. I know your daughter, Mr. Culver, and I'm sure she has *nothing* to do with anti-American propaganda."

Propaganda. There was that word again.

Molly wasn't sure what it meant. She *did* know that *anti-American* meant "against America." Which wasn't good. Germany was anti-American.

"You bet she had nothing to do with it," Granpa retorted. "This is my *daughter* we're talking about, not some enemy spy. Do you have any idea where the FBI agents are taking her?"

"No. But I'm sure Miss Culver will be released just as soon as they finish questioning her. I'll call you if I hear anything."

Time to scoot. Molly sprinted down the hall, out the front doors, and across the field toward the planes.

Someone wearing tan coveralls was standing beside the P-51. *Aunt Eleanor!* Molly was about to call out her name when she realized it was only a mechanic. Her heart sank.

When she reached the pickup, she opened the door and climbed in. She slumped in the hot seat, one thought swirling through her head: *Aunt Eleanor is really gone!*

★

Granpa was silent the whole way home.

"You run along and play," he said to Molly when he had parked the pickup under the oak. "Your grandmother and I have things to discuss."

"Yes, sir," Molly said quickly. She'd been hoping to be dismissed. She ran to the barn and pulled out her bike. She wanted to get to the Schulzes' as soon as possible. She wanted to tell Anna about the FBI taking Aunt Eleanor.

Molly knew Anna would care about what was happening to Aunt Eleanor. *And maybe now, Anna will talk about what's happening to her family, too.*

The bike ride over was hot and dusty. Molly spotted Anna in the shade of the barn, scattering corn to the chickens. She wore Molly's Camp Gowonagin cap.

Molly jumped off her bike and let it fall to the ground. Without a hello, she launched into her tale.

As Molly talked, Anna's mouth fell open. The bucket of corn dropped from her grasp. Eyes wide, she glanced toward the house. Then, out of the blue, she grabbed Molly's hand and pulled her behind the barn. "Come on. Let's go to the trash pile," she said, her voice lowered. "We can talk there."

Molly hurried after her. They made their way down the weedy path to the old trash pile. It was half-hidden by dirt, leaves, rusty tractor parts, and brambles.

Breathless, Anna turned to face Molly. "Tell me again about the FBI men," she demanded. "Tell me again what they looked like."

Molly described them.

"Those are the same two that came to our farm, all right." Frowning, Anna chewed on a ragged fingernail. "What could it mean?"

Molly dropped her gaze. Stooping, she absently dug through the trash with a stick. She knew she had to tell Anna what she'd heard about Max. "Mr. Kay said that the FBI agents have been checking around the airfield. And, um, Aunt Eleanor said that Mr. Kay is being pressured to fire Max because he's German."

Anna burst out, "German! That's what the FBI men kept saying when they ransacked our house. But Molly, Max and I have never even been to Germany!"

"Wait a minute," Molly said. "The FBI ransacked your house?" She jumped to her feet. *"That's* why they were here yesterday?"

Anna nodded, a miserable expression on her face. Picking up an old can, she threw it at a tree trunk. It clattered loudly.

"What were they looking for?" Molly asked.

"Papa sent me to the barn when they came. But later he told me they were looking for contraband."

"What's that?" Molly asked.

"Papa said contraband could be guns used for fighting Americans. Or two-way radios for contacting German spies. Or anti-American propaganda like they found in your Aunt Eleanor's plane."

This time Molly's mouth fell open. "In *your* house?"

"Yes, isn't that silly?" Anna said, but her voice cracked and she began to cry. "Molly, it's just like what happened to the Kruegers. And they got sent away to one of those camps!"

"Oh, Anna, don't cry." Molly put her arm around her friend's shoulder. "Gosh, both of our families are in trouble."

"Mine is in trouble because Mama and Papa are German," Anna said between sobs. "But Molly, not all Germans are bad. My grandmama and grandpapa live in Germany. They run a bakery. They're not soldiers or spies."

Molly nodded.

"I *knew* something bad was going to happen," Anna said, wiping away a tear. "After Papa and Mama got the letter from the Kruegers, they whispered late into the night. I crept by their bedroom and heard them say something about other German friends in America who were taken away by the FBI and put in camps. Oh, Molly, what if we're taken, too? I don't want to leave my home!"

An ache filled Molly's chest. She had no idea how to help Anna.

"If the FBI comes to take you away, I'll tell them that you're as loyal to America as I am," Molly said. "I'll tell them how Max wants to be a pilot for the Army, and how you wanted to collect cans for the war effort."

But even Molly wasn't reassured by her words. How could she help Anna and her family? She'd been *right there* when the FBI had taken her aunt, and she hadn't been able to do a thing about it.

6
A HIDDEN CLUE

"But Granpa, I want to go with you,"
Molly pleaded as she followed him to the
pickup. Last night they hadn't heard from
Eleanor. This morning, Granpa was driving
into Weston to see if he could find out any
news.

"No, Miss Molly, you cannot come with
me," Granpa said, opening the truck door.
"You stay and help Grammy." He bent toward
Molly and whispered, "She's pretty upset and
needs your support."

"Yes, sir." Molly stepped away from the
truck. Silently, she watched Granpa drive
away. *Oh, I hate being left behind!* she thought.

"Molly!" Grammy called from the back
porch. "Come get your straw hat and bucket.

We'd best pick berries before the day heats up."

Sighing, Molly joined Grammy, who seemed convinced that a morning of berry-picking would ease their minds. As they hiked into the field behind the Culvers' barn, Grammy kept up a stream of nervous chatter. "Oh, look at the wild roses. And over there is a bluebird! My, I haven't seen a bluebird all summer."

At the edge of the woods, they found blackberry bushes bursting with dark fruit. "Land sakes, these will make enough jam for four families!" Grammy exclaimed. "I can send a jar home with you, Molly. And send a jar to the Schulzes and . . ."

As Grammy talked on, Molly replied "umm-hmm" and "golly" until finally the hot sun wore her grandmother into silence. For over an hour they picked berries. When their buckets were full, they headed home.

As they rounded the side of the barn, Molly heard the grind of a truck motor. "It's

Granpa!" She broke into a run, the heavy bucket banging against her leg. Blackberries spilled to the ground. Granpa parked the truck, and Aunt Eleanor climbed out from the passenger side.

"Yippeee!" Molly cheered. Setting down the bucket, she rushed to her aunt and wrapped her arms around her.

Seconds later, Grammy joined them in the hug. Pulling away, Molly looked up into her aunt's face. Dark shadows circled Eleanor's blue eyes, and her brown curls were matted. She still wore her zoot suit.

Molly took her aunt's duffel bag from the truck bed. "Gosh, did they question you all night? Where did they take you? Did they put you in a jail cell? What did they want?" Molly's questions tumbled out as they walked to the back porch.

"Hush, young lady," Granpa scolded. "Your aunt's exhausted. Let her be."

"It's all right, Dad," Aunt Eleanor said, stepping onto the back porch. "Molly has a right to answers."

"After you rest," Grammy said.

"No, I need to tell her now. You all need to know." Aunt Eleanor turned and faced them. "The FBI agents questioned me about the leaflets found in the plane. But mostly they asked me about Max and Mr. Schulz." Her eyes reddened with tears. "This morning, Max was arrested."

Grammy pressed her fingers against her lips. Molly gasped, "Why?"

"The FBI believes that Max belongs to an anti-American group called the Silver Legion," Eleanor went on. "They think that he's the one at the airfield who's smuggling the propaganda leaflets."

"For crying out loud!" Molly exclaimed. "Max wouldn't do something anti-American!" she protested, echoing Mr. Kay's words about Eleanor. "Um, what exactly is propaganda?"

"It's a way to spread opinions *for* or *against* something," Aunt Eleanor explained. "All the armies use propaganda: British, German, American. Sending messages to the enemy to 'give up' or 'surrender' is one way to win the war."

"What did the propaganda leaflets in your plane say?" Molly asked, stepping onto the porch next to her aunt.

"They said that America should give up the fight against Germany," Aunt Eleanor replied. "The FBI thinks the leaflets were being smuggled to an air base in Texas where many pilots and soldiers are in training. Whoever is smuggling the leaflets must be trying to turn our soldiers against their own country."

"I've never heard of such balderdash," Granpa muttered.

"Why would the FBI suspect *Max* of something like that?" Grammy asked Aunt Eleanor. "He's just a boy."

"Max serviced the plane early yesterday morning," Aunt Eleanor said. "The FBI agents believe that he hid the leaflets in the wing when he filled the fuel tank and checked the tires. The FBI suspects that another member of the Silver Legion would pick up the leaflets after my plane landed in Texas."

"What is the Silver Legion?" Molly asked.

"Nothing a young lady like you should know about," Granpa said firmly.

Aunt Eleanor leaned over so that she was eye-to-eye with Molly. "They are an anti-American group, which means they support our enemies. Before the war, they were very active. They held rallies against President Roosevelt. They called themselves the Silver Shirts because sometimes they paraded in cities wearing silver-colored shirts with a bright red L on the front. The L stands for Love, Loyalty, and Liberation. But as noble as those words sound, the Silver Legion is against our government."

"Why would Max belong to a group like that?"

"Max *wouldn't* belong to a group like that." Aunt Eleanor straightened. "And that's what I told agents Platt and Danvers. I told them the Schulzes are fine people. I told them Max dreams of being a pilot in the Army Air Force. *That's* why he works at the airfield—not because he's smuggling propaganda leaflets. But the agents wouldn't listen," she added bitterly.

"Now, now, dear," Grammy soothed. "You're tired and hungry. Maybe things will look better after you rest. Let's go inside and get something to eat. I'll bet those FBI fellows didn't feed you." She held open the screen door.

Molly watched as Aunt Eleanor followed Grammy and Granpa inside. She was relieved that Eleanor was home, yet she couldn't stop thinking about Max.

Mr. and Mrs. Schulz will be worried sick, Molly thought. *And poor Anna!* Molly left the duffel bag on the porch and ran to find her bike.

She had to see Anna, and help her if she could.

Molly pedaled quickly to the farm. Anna

was sitting on the porch steps, her head propped in her hands. When she saw Molly, she jumped up.

"Molly, did you hear about Max? He's been arrested!" Anna cried. Molly could see the tear streaks on her friend's face.

"Aunt Eleanor told me." Without slowing the bike, Molly dismounted and ran toward Anna, pushing the bike along by the handlebars. "I'm so sorry, Anna."

Anna took a shaky breath but nodded bravely. "Is your aunt okay? Did she know anything more about Max?"

"Let's go to the pond, and I'll tell you what she said." Molly dropped her bike in the grass. She grabbed Anna's hand, and the two girls ran past the barn and down the path. The whole bike ride over to the farm, Molly had been thinking about how to help Max. She had an idea, and she wanted to tell Anna in private.

When they reached the pond, the girls plopped onto the end of the dock. The afternoon sun shimmered on the still, green water. It was so hot that even the frogs were silent.

Molly took off her Keds and dangled her legs over the end of the dock. As she swished her feet in the water, she told Anna what Aunt Eleanor had said. Anna just stared at her.

"Max? A Silver Shirt?" Anna repeated when Molly had finished talking. "That's the silliest thing I ever heard."

"I know," Molly agreed. "And it all sounds scary, but Anna, we can help Max."

"How are *we* going to help Max?" Anna asked. "We're just *kids*."

"So what?" Molly protested. "We can go to the airfield and look for clues to figure out who's *really* guilty."

Anna shot Molly an impatient look. "This isn't *I Love a Mystery*, Molly. Max getting arrested is *real*."

"You don't have to remind me," Molly said soberly. "But we can prove to those agents that Max is innocent. All we have to do is find the real Silver Shirt who hid those leaflets."

"Oh, *that* should be a cinch," Anna scoffed. "Why, we'll just ask everybody who works at the airfield. 'Excuse me,'" she said in a faked gruff voice, "'are you the person who hid propaganda leaflets in Miss Culver's plane?'"

"Don't be silly, Anna." Molly kicked up sprays of water, cooling her bare legs. "It's not *that* easy. But you're right, the bad guy could be anyone at the airfield."

"That's true." Anna chewed on her bottom lip and frowned as if thinking hard. "The mechanics would know about hiding places in the planes. And the men who work in the tower would know your aunt's flight plan. They'd know she was flying to Texas."

Molly pulled her dripping feet from the water. "Let's ride our bikes to the airfield. We'll hunt for clues."

Anna still looked doubtful.

"Come on, Anna," Molly urged. "We'll never help Max if we don't try."

"You know what? You're right." Anna

jumped up, suddenly eager. "My bike's in the barn."

Grabbing their shoes, the two girls ran up the path. Minutes later, they were on their way to the airfield, pedaling hard down Route 11. Whenever a car passed, Molly held her breath, afraid it might be Granpa or someone they knew. Finally they turned onto the lane leading to the airfield. Halfway down the lane, they stopped and hid their bikes in the tall grass.

"Let's go this way," Molly said, leading the way through the weeds. "It's best if no one sees us snooping around."

The two girls stopped when they reached the mowed airfield. Squinting in the sun, Molly scanned the row of parked planes. She spotted the P-51, exactly where it had been when the FBI agents took Aunt Eleanor away.

"There's no one around, Anna. Follow me." Molly ran across the field. When she reached the P-51, she hunkered down beside the tail.

Anna knelt beside her. "This is the plane your aunt was flying?"

Molly nodded. "Isn't it a beaut?"

"So what's your plan?"

"First, I want to check out where the leaflets were hidden. The *real* Silver Shirt may have left a clue behind." Molly peered around the plane's tail. When she was sure no one was nearby, she slipped over to the back of the left wing, with Anna right behind her.

"The one FBI agent said the stacks of leaflets were hidden in the 'ammunition receptacle,'" Molly explained. "I'm not sure what that is, but the agent pointed to a panel in the middle of this wing."

Molly found the wooden block that she and Aunt Eleanor had used to step up onto the plane. She dragged it over and then stood on it so that she could see the top of the wing. Tilting her head, she tried to figure out how to open the panel. She found two levers. When she pushed down on them, the panel popped open. She lifted it up. Inside the wing was a rectangular space about six inches deep.

"What a nifty hiding place," Molly said, gesturing for Anna to step up and look.

Anna climbed up on the wooden block. "It sure is. But I don't see any clues."

Molly carefully checked the space. The sun illuminated every corner, but she didn't see anything that might be a clue. "I bet the A-1 Detectives carry a magnifying glass."

"Well, *we* don't have one." Anna glanced around nervously. "And we'd better scram before someone spots us. I'll get into big trouble if my parents find out I was snooping around the airfield."

"Me, too." Molly reached up to close the panel. "Wait. What's this?"

"What's what?"

Molly looked closely at the underside of the panel. "There *is* a clue! Smudges of oil. Like fingerprints."

"I see them, too!"

"Anna, does Max work on the plane engines?"

"No. He just checks the tires and fills up the gas."

"This is definitely oil. Granpa gets it all over himself when he works on the truck motor." Excitement rushed through Molly. "The oil must mean that a mechanic, not Max, opened up this panel and stuck those leaflets in the wing!" Closing the panel, she pushed down 106 to latch it.

"Oh, Molly, do you really think so?" Anna asked as the two jumped off the wooden block.

"I *know* so. Why else would a mechanic be looking in the ammunition receptacle? There's no motor to fix in there."

Anna wrung her hands together. "I don't know. It seems too easy. Why didn't the FBI agents find the oil? Why didn't *they* question the mechanics?" Her expression darkened with anger. "Wait, I know. They were *too busy* arresting my brother because our parents are German!" Suddenly, Anna looked over Molly's shoulder and her eyes grew wide. "Someone's coming!"

A Hidden Clue

Molly whipped around. Two men wearing mechanics' coveralls were approaching the parked planes. Any second they'd spot the girls.

Molly grabbed Anna's hand. "Quick," she hissed urgently, "we have to hide!"

7
AN A-1 DETECTIVE

"Under here!" Molly pulled Anna beneath the wing and into the deep shadow cast by the body of the plane. She could hear voices approaching. As the voices grew louder, Molly shot Anna a frightened look.

Seconds later, two pairs of coverall-clad legs walked past the plane and kept going. Molly held her breath. When the voices faded to silence, she exhaled with relief.

"Whew. *That* was a close shave," she said as they crawled out from under the wing.

"*Too* close for me." Anna glanced in the direction the men had gone. "I don't want to be a detective anymore, Molly."

"Okay," Molly agreed quickly. She'd been so scared, her pulse was still racing. "Let's bike home and tell Aunt Eleanor about the fingerprints. She'll know what to do."

"*You* tell Eleanor," Anna said as she brushed off her dirt-covered bottom. "Mama's upset enough about Max. I don't want her to find out that I snuck off."

Molly crinkled her nose. "I didn't tell Grammy we were biking to the airfield, either."

"Then we'd better am-scray," Anna said. "Or we'll both be grounded. Then neither of us will be able to help Max!"

★

An hour later, Molly rushed into Grammy's kitchen. She was sweaty and dusty from the long bike ride home. Grammy was slicing carrots and potatoes on a cutting board.

"Where's Aunt Eleanor?" Molly asked.

"And good evening to you, too," Grammy teased. "Where have you been all afternoon?"

"Um, I was riding bikes with Anna. Is Aunt Eleanor around?"

"She's resting." Grammy glanced over at Molly. "That must have been some bike ride. Your pants are covered with grass stains."

"Oh, uh, we did some hiking, too," Molly said. She hated to fib, but she didn't dare tell Grammy she'd been sneaking around the airfield.

"Well, wash up and change your clothes. By the way, your mother telephoned. I'm sorry you missed her call."

"What did she want? Is everybody okay?"

"She'll be here Sunday afternoon to pick you up. The whole family's coming."

"Sunday! But that's only two days from now!"

Grammy set the knife on the cutting board. "Why, I thought you'd be pleased," she said, turning toward Molly. "I know you've missed your family. And school starts a week after you get home. You'll need to get your school outfits together and buy your supplies. My, to think of it, you'll be starting a brand-new school year!"

Molly *had* missed her family. And she *was*

excited about school. But would two days be enough time to save Max?

"Well, go ahead and wake your aunt," Grammy said. "Tell her it'll soon be supper-time. Then I need you to set the table. But don't forget to wash up first," she added as Molly rushed from the kitchen.

Molly took the stairs in two's. Quickly, she washed her hands, splashed water on her face, and changed into clean shorts and shirt. While still buttoning her shirt, she dashed into Eleanor's room.

The curtains were closed, but her aunt's eyes were open.

"Oh, good," Molly said. "You're awake."

"An elephant clumping around the bath-room woke me."

"Sorry." Molly giggled. "Grammy said to tell you supper's almost ready." Unable to contain her excitement, she blurted, "Anna and I think a mechanic hid those leaflets, not Max! We can prove it, too. We—" She stopped abruptly.

Aunt Eleanor had propped her head on one arm. She was staring at Molly, and the expression on her face reminded Molly of Granpa.

Molly gulped. *I can't tell her I was at the airfield!*

Aunt Eleanor was her friend. But she was still a grownup. Molly knew what her aunt would say. *You cannot go to the airfield without supervision. And you certainly can't snoop around the planes!*

Eleanor sat up and swung her legs over the side of the bed. "How can you prove Max is innocent?" she asked quietly. "This isn't a Nancy Drew mystery, you know."

"I know," Molly replied. "It's a lot more serious than that." She felt a rush of emotion. "Anna and I are just really worried about Max. Her whole family's worried! So we thought we'd try to prove that Max is innocent. We decided that since the mechanics work around the planes, one of *them* could be the Silver Shirt. One of *them* could have hidden those leaflets."

Aunt Eleanor walked over to her dresser. "Molly, I understand why you're trying to help Max," she said as she brushed her hair. "But this is a complicated matter. Max's arrest is a mistake, but you let the grownups help the Schulzes." She glanced at Molly in the mirror.

Molly dove belly-first onto Aunt Eleanor's bed. "Do *you* think it could be a mechanic?"

Aunt Eleanor set down the brush and looked at Molly over her shoulder. "Probably not. Dave and George are the only mechanics who have enough skill to work on army fighter planes. But neither was authorized to work on the P-51. Besides, if they're going to work on a plane, they taxi it into the hangar."

Dave and George. Molly tapped her lip in thought. *I bet one of them is a member of the Silver Legion.* She wished she could get back to the airfield and find out more about them. But there were only two days before she had to go home. Would she be able to sneak away again? Would there be time for the long bike ride there and back?

"Tomorrow Granpa's driving me to the airfield," Aunt Eleanor said. "Early. Will you come and see me off?"

Molly was about to say yes when an idea hit her. *That's how I can get to the airfield. I'll hide in the back of Granpa's truck.* When he was busy saying good-bye to Aunt Eleanor, she could slip into the hangar where Dave and George worked and look around.

"Gosh, I'm sorry, Aunt Eleanor. I, um, have some things to do tomorrow morning," she said.

Molly bit her lip. She felt awful misleading Aunt Eleanor. But Anna had been so hopeful when they'd found the greasy prints. Molly *couldn't* stop investigating now.

★

Early the next morning, the pickup rattled and banged down the Culvers' lane. Molly, hidden under feed sacks and scrunched between hay bales, bounced in the truck bed. The sacks were musty, and the metal floor smelled like gasoline. She held her nose, afraid of sneezing.

Last night, Molly and Anna had met at the swimming hole. The Schulzes had no news about Max. Molly had filled Anna in on her plan. "Oh, I hope you can find something that will help Max," her friend had said. "I want my brother home!"

This morning, as the sun was rising, Molly had kissed Aunt Eleanor good-bye. Then, telling Grammy she'd be back in a while, she'd slipped off to the shed where the pickup was parked. She'd hidden under the sacks and waited for Granpa and Aunt Eleanor.

The truck stopped and the motor shut off. "I'll meet you by the P-51, Dad," Molly heard her aunt say. "I've got to file my flight plan. And I want to talk to Mr. Kay about Max."

Perfect, Molly thought. She'd have time to look around. She could hide again in the truck bed for the ride home. No one would know she'd ever been at the airfield.

When she was sure Granpa and Eleanor were gone, Molly peeked from under the feed sacks. Cautiously, she raised her head. Granpa had parked under a tree close to the brick terminal. The hangar where the mechanics worked was off to the right. It was Molly's destination.

She scanned the airfield. Since it was early, the airport wasn't busy. She spotted Granpa by the P-51, and there were a few cars in the gravel parking lot, but she didn't see any people milling about.

Here's my chance. Throwing back the sacks, Molly crawled over a hay bale and jumped from the truck bed. She raced toward the planes parked in the cleared area in front of the open hangar doors. Kneeling beside a tire, she peered into the building. *Is anyone inside?* she wondered.

Lights were suspended from the ceiling, but they were off and the building was fairly dark. Molly could make out the shape of a plane parked in the center of the hangar. Parts were scattered on the dirt floor around the plane. The rest of the hangar was shadowy and quiet.

It didn't seem as if anyone was inside. But Molly guessed that the mechanics would soon arrive for work.

She glanced over her shoulder. A car was pulling into the parking lot in front of the terminal. She had to act now—the airfield might soon be crawling with people.

Jumping up, Molly raced inside the hangar and dropped down in the right-hand corner behind a ladder. Her heart thumped. She waited, expecting someone to holler, but her detective instincts were right—no one was in the hangar.

As Molly's eyes adjusted to the dim interior, she checked out the cavernous hangar. Along the walls were wooden bins and shelves filled with tools. There was one doorway located in the right-hand wall. A sign over the door frame said "Locker Room." Dave, George, and the other mechanics probably kept their belongings there, Molly guessed. It would be a good place to start looking for clues.

Molly glanced over her shoulder one more time to make sure no one was coming, then dashed for the locker-room door. She hesitated, her hand on the knob. Her stomach tightened. What if someone was inside? She put her ear against the door, listening. When she didn't hear anything, she pushed open the door, slipped inside, and shut it quickly behind her.

I did it! Relieved, she sagged against the closed door. But there was no time to waste.

Molly scanned the small room. It was lit by a narrow window high in the wall to her right. In front of her, a dozen upright gray metal lockers lined the back wall. To her left, against the wall opposite the lockers, stood a wide wooden bench. The only door was the one behind her, leading back into the hangar.

Stepping closer to the lockers, Molly saw

that each was labeled with a name written on paper and tucked into a slot in the door. Quickly, she walked down the row until she found Dave's and George's lockers. Would they be locked?

She tried George's locker first and was surprised when it opened. A pair of olive green coveralls hung from a hook. She stuck her hand into the pockets, hoping for a clue that would point her in the direction of the *real* Silver Shirt. All she found was a wadded-up gum wrapper. She shut the locker door, jumping when it clanked noisily.

Holding her breath, she listened for sounds from the hangar. *Silence.* Her heartbeat slowed, and she opened the locker that said "Dave."

Another pair of olive green coveralls hung from a hook. Quickly, she checked the pockets. *Empty.* A wave of disappointment filled her. Then she noticed something on the floor of Dave's locker, half-hidden under the legs of the coveralls.

Molly crouched down. It was a black metal lunch box. She flipped up the latch and raised the domed lid. Tucked inside was a pile of yellow, postcard-sized leaflets printed with American flags.

Molly sucked in her breath. *They look just like the leaflets found in Aunt Eleanor's plane!*

She pulled a leaflet from the lunch box and smoothed it out. An American flag was printed in color at the top of the leaflet. Molly flipped the leaflet over, and her eyes widened. A picture in the middle of the page showed a young man in a silver shirt, and he was carrying a white flag emblazoned with a scarlet L. The words on the card declared: "Soldiers, Rise Up Against America. Rise Up Against Roosevelt. Do Not Die in a War That's Not Yours!"

Molly felt a surge of anger. *So this is anti-American propaganda.* No wonder the FBI didn't want the Silver Shirts smuggling these leaflets to air bases. They were telling American soldiers to give up the fight!

"We've got to fix the vertical stabilizer on that left rudder—"

Molly tensed. *Voices.* Someone was coming!

8
A Close Call

Molly shoved the leaflet into her pocket and stood up. Carefully, she closed the locker door, trying not to make a sound.

"I'll work on it once I get that altimeter adjusted."

The voices were right outside the door. Pulse racing, Molly surveyed the small room. There was no good place to hide.

The doorknob rattled. Dropping to the floor, Molly slid under the wooden bench at the same instant the door opened. Light shone into the room. She pressed against the wall, pushing herself as far out of sight as possible.

Staring from her hiding place, Molly saw three pairs of work boots walk in. She froze. She heard locker doors opening. As the men moved around, they talked about carburetor heat and fuselage tanks.

Molly closed her eyes and buried her head in her crossed arms. The frames of her glasses poked into her cheeks. She didn't dare breathe.

Finally, the lockers clanged shut. Molly peeked from under her elbow.

"I wonder where Frank and Dave are," one of the men said as the three pairs of work boots strode from the locker room.

Dave! Molly swallowed the lump in her throat. Any minute he might come into the locker room. *I've got to get out of here!*

Trying to keep her hands from shaking, Molly righted her glasses and eased away from the wall. Slowly she poked her head from under the bench. The men had left the door cracked open. She listened. She could hear their voices echoing through the hangar.

Molly groaned silently. Sneaking *out* would be much trickier than sneaking *in*. But it was too risky to stay a second longer.

She crawled from under the bench. Her shirt and shorts were covered with dust. She brushed herself off and pushed the leaflet deeper into her pocket. Then she eased open the door and peeked out.

The overhead lights were on. Molly's gaze moved around the hangar until she'd located all three mechanics. One was on top of the plane's wing. One was under the wing. The third was pulling parts from a wooden box. No one was looking her way.

Molly chewed her lip, afraid to make a move. What if one of them noticed her? How would she explain coming out of the locker room?

Come on, Molly, you've got to get going, she told herself. *Anna and Max are counting on you!*

She took a shaky breath, then murmured, "One, two, three—*go*." She launched herself from the room. Hunched over, she scurried along the wall toward the open doors, hugging the shadows. She was glad she'd worn denim shorts and a navy blue blouse. Only her white socks stood out.

Silently, she slipped past the ladder and hurried from the hangar. When the sunlight hit her, she glanced over her shoulder. No one was running after her. No one called for her to halt. *I made it!*

Whack! Molly slammed hard into something. The force knocked her backward. She landed on her bottom. Her glasses flew off her head.

"Oh, gosh. Sorry, miss!" someone said.

A young man squatted next to her. Molly peered at him. Without her glasses his face looked fuzzy, but she could see that he was wearing olive green coveralls.

"Sorry," he apologized again. "You were coming out of the hangar so fast, you ran smack into me. Here." He held out her glasses. "They're not broken."

"Th–thanks," Molly stammered as she slid them on. The young man popped into focus. He was stocky, with a pleasant smile and a crew cut.

"Hey, aren't you Eleanor Culver's niece?"

"Um, yes." Molly ducked her chin. She didn't dare look up. One glimpse of her guilty face and he would know she'd been snooping in the hangar.

"I bet you came to watch her take off in that P-51, huh?"

"Uh, right, yes, that's exactly why I'm here," Molly agreed quickly.

"I'm Dave. One of the mechanics."

Dave! Heat flooded Molly's face.

"I know your aunt pretty well," he went on, motioning toward the runway. "Better hurry. She's about to take off."

"Th–thanks." Molly scrambled to her feet and started to hurry away.

"Say hi to your grandparents for me," Dave called.

Molly gave him a backward wave. Sweat broke out under her bangs. *That's Dave— the one who has the leaflets stashed in his locker! The one who must have put the propaganda in Aunt Eleanor's plane!*

She broke into a run, her hand instinctively

covering her pocket. She could feel the outline of the leaflet through the fabric.

Directly overhead, a plane roared by. Molly slowed and shaded her eyes. The plane banked right, and she spotted a star in the middle of a blue circle. She waved, even though her aunt was too far away to see.

Heading off again, Molly quickly reached the parking lot. By now, it was half-full, but she didn't see Granpa's pickup truck.

Molly turned in a circle, double-checking. The truck wasn't parked under the tree *or* by the planes. It wasn't *anywhere*. Granpa had left, too.

For a minute, Molly stood and stared, not sure what to do. Then her hand clenched the leaflet in her pocket.

I've got to show this to someone, Molly thought. But who could she turn to? Aunt Eleanor was on the way to Texas. And Granpa would be furious with her for sneaking around.

Molly tugged at her braid, thinking hard. She couldn't give the leaflet to Mr. Schulz, either—the FBI might use it as proof against him. And she couldn't take it to the FBI agents. She didn't know how to find them, and besides, the agents would never believe a kid.

Molly paced beside a delivery truck. She had to give the leaflet to *someone.* It proved that Dave was a Silver Shirt. She was sure that Dave, not Max, had hidden the leaflets in Aunt Eleanor's plane. But the evidence was worthless unless someone showed the leaflet to the FBI agents.

Someone in authority. Someone who could convince the FBI of Max's innocence.

Someone like Mr. Kay!

Molly felt a wave of relief. Why hadn't she thought of Mr. Kay before? Hadn't he offered to help when the FBI agents had taken Aunt Eleanor?

Clutching the leaflet in her pocket, Molly raced into the terminal and down the hall. She burst into Mr. Kay's office without stopping to knock.

Startled, Mr. Kay shot from his desk chair.

"What is the meaning of this, young lady?"

"I'm sorry for barging in," Molly said breathlessly. "I'm Molly McIntire, Eleanor Culver's niece, and I have proof that Max is innocent!"

Mr. Kay stared at her, his moustache a stiff line over his lips.

Molly pulled the leaflet from her pocket and thrust it toward him. "Look at this! I found it in the hangar—in *Dave's* locker!" Mr. Kay took the leaflet gingerly and examined it as Molly quickly explained how she'd discovered it. As Molly talked, he glanced from her face to the leaflet with an astonished expression.

"Why, that's incredible, Miss McIntire," he said when she finished. "And you're right. This is identical to the leaflets found in your aunt's plane. I'll make sure that Agents Platt and Danvers get it immediately."

"Thank you!" Molly exclaimed, glad that she'd come to the right person. "But what about Dave?" she asked. "I don't want him to get away."

Mr. Kay pointed the leaflet at her. "You

let the FBI handle Dave. You're in enough trouble for sneaking into that locker room."

Molly winced. "Oh, gosh, you won't tell Granpa, will you? *Please* don't tell him."

For a minute, Mr. Kay furrowed his brow. Then he nodded. "How about if I tell the FBI agents that *I* discovered the leaflet? That way you won't get into trouble, Miss McIntire."

"Thank you." Molly looked up at Mr. Kay and smiled. "For *everything.* The Schulzes will be so happy when Max comes home!"

"Thank *you,* Miss McIntire." Mr. Kay came around the desk and shook hands with Molly. "You know, I never thought Max was guilty, either."

Molly said good-bye and left the office. As she walked down the hall, she felt lighter than air. *Wait until I tell Anna!*

But only Anna, Molly reminded herself. Anna would keep the secret of how Molly had sneaked into the hangar to find the evidence.

Molly left the terminal and stepped out into the bright sunshine. Maybe she could never tell anyone except Anna how she had helped Max. And maybe she faced a long, hot walk back to the farm. But she didn't care. Soon the FBI agents would release Max, and Anna's wish would come true: Her brother would be home and safe!

★

That evening, Molly waited for Grammy and Granpa's phone to ring. She curled up in an armchair in the living room, her Nancy Drew mystery in her lap. She tried to read, but her eyes kept straying to the silent phone on the wall.

By now Mr. Kay had taken the leaflet to the FBI. By now the agents must have let Max go. Why hadn't Anna or her parents called with the good news?

By eight o'clock, Molly was tired of waiting. Jumping up, she picked up the receiver and tapped the button on the phone.

"Operator. Number, please," a nasal voice sang out.

Molly gave the operator Anna's number and the operator put the call through to the Schulzes. Anna answered on the first ring.

"Anna, hi! Has there been any news about Max?"

"No." Anna replied. "Papa couldn't even see him at the county jail."

Quickly Molly told her about finding the leaflet and taking it to Mr. Kay.

"But then why are the FBI agents still holding Max?" Anna sounded upset.

"I don't know," Molly said. "The FBI agents should have released him."

A moment later, Grammy came into the living room. Molly said good-bye to Anna and hung up.

"Any news?" Grammy asked.

Molly shook her head angrily. "Anna said Max is still at the jail. The FBI won't let Mr. Schulz even talk to him. It's not fair!" She sat down in the chair and pounded the armrest with her fist.

"Sometimes life isn't fair, sweetheart."

Grammy stroked Molly's hair. "Maybe there will be good news tomorrow. Your Aunt Eleanor will be here by early afternoon. That's something to look forward to, and things *always* look brighter in the morning."

Molly sighed dejectedly.

"I know, how would you like to go out to the barn and see the new calf?" Grammy suggested brightly.

Molly shook her head. "No, thank you." She stood up, her book in her hand. "I'm going to bed." She kissed Grammy good night and trudged up the stairs. She hoped Grammy was right. She hoped that things *would* be brighter in the morning.

★

"Eleanor's arriving around noon," Grammy told Molly the next morning. Molly was seated at the kitchen table eating peaches sliced on Kellogg's Cornflakes. "Granpa's driving to the airfield to pick her up."

Molly nodded, her mouth full.

"I talked to the Schulzes this morning," Grammy added as she rinsed dishes in the sink. "There's still no news about Max."

Molly gulped down her cornflakes. "How can that *be?* We all know Max is innocent."

"These things take time. But Eleanor will help, too—she told Granpa that she wants to go directly from the airfield to the jail. She hopes to help Mr. Schulz sort out this mess." Grammy sighed. Suds dripped from her fingers. "Your granpa's torn. He wants to help our neighbors, but he doesn't want Eleanor involved."

Molly kept her eyes on her bowl. Part of her wanted to tell Grammy about Dave, the leaflet, and Mr. Kay. But she held back.

Abruptly, she stood up. "I'm biking over to Anna's to see how she's doing."

"You're a good friend, Molly." Grammy smiled. "Get going. I'll wash your dishes for you."

Molly handed her the bowl and spoon,

then gave Grammy an unexpected hug.

"My, that's nice." Grammy held her close. "I think someone misses her family."

Molly wished she could tell Grammy the real reason she was so blue. "Yeah, I do. Well, maybe not *Ricky*," she added, trying to make Grammy smile again.

Outside, Molly raced to the barn, mounted her bike, and pedaled up the lane. *Gotta hurry, gotta hurry, gotta hurry* rang through her head with each spin of the tires. When she reached Route 11, she spotted Anna pedaling toward her, the Camp Gowonagin cap pulled securely on her head.

"I was coming over to see you," Anna said breathlessly as she stopped at the end of the Culvers' lane. "I couldn't stand waiting around with Mama."

Molly dismounted. "I know what you mean."

"I don't understand what's going on!" Anna exclaimed. "Why isn't Max home?"

"I don't know. Aunt Eleanor's flying in today. Grammy said she's going straight to the jail where they're holding Max. But Anna, we need to do something *now*. I'm going home tomorrow, so we can't waste any more time." Molly got back on her bike. "Let's go talk to Mr. Kay," she said as she pushed off. "We need to find out what the FBI agents said when he gave them that leaflet."

This time, the girls rode straight to the terminal, parking their bikes under a huge oak tree. "Why don't you stay here while I talk to Mr. Kay?" Molly suggested. "He might tell me more if I talk to him alone."

Anna nodded. "I'll wait for you right here."

Molly headed into the building and down the hall. The door to the manager's office was open. Molly peered inside. "Mr. Kay?"

Molly spotted his navy suit jacket hanging on a coatrack by the door, but the manager wasn't in his office. She wanted to kick the doorjamb in frustration. *Oh, where is he?*

She was turning to leave when she noticed a triangle of yellow paper sticking from Mr. Kay's jacket pocket. Molly froze.

She checked the hall to make sure no one was coming and then tiptoed closer. Carefully, she grasped the corner of the paper and tugged it halfway out of the coat pocket.

Molly stared at the yellow paper. It was the propaganda leaflet, *and it was still in Mr. Kay's pocket.*

9
ON THE TRAIL

Molly's heart dropped. Hadn't the FBI agents believed Mr. Kay—had they just sent him away? Or hadn't Mr. Kay even taken the leaflet to them yet? But that couldn't be, Molly told herself. Yesterday he'd said he was taking it to the agents *immediately*.

Sliding the leaflet back into the coat pocket, Molly rushed down the hall to look for Mr. Kay. There were several people in the lobby but no one she recognized. She went up to a gray-haired woman seated at a typewriter.

"Excuse me, do you know where Mr. Kay is?" she asked the secretary.

The woman peered at her through her glasses. "No, miss. May I help you with something?"

"No, thank you." Molly stepped away from the desk. Hurrying outside, she stopped on the terminal steps. Anna stood under the tree, an expectant look on her face. Molly wished she had good news for her friend.

She glanced toward the hangar. *What about Dave?* she wondered. Had Mr. Kay even told the FBI about the *real* Silver Shirt?

Suddenly Molly spotted a man walking toward the terminal from the direction of the hangar. He had slicked-back hair and wore a light blue shirt. *Mr. Kay.*

Maybe the manager had gone to confront Dave!

Molly leaped down the steps and ran over to Anna. "Come on, there's Mr. Kay now. Let's go talk to him."

Taking Anna's hand, she started toward the hangar. When she reached the edge of the parking lot, she stopped in confusion. Mr. Kay was nowhere in sight.

"Why'd you stop?" Anna asked. "Where's Mr. Kay?"

"I thought he was headed toward the terminal," Molly said. "Now I don't see him. Maybe there's a back entrance into the building—Hey, wait!"

Just then, Molly caught sight of a second man striding from the hangar. He wore olive green coveralls, and his brown hair was styled in a crew cut. *Dave.*

Molly watched as Dave turned sharply and headed down the left side of the hangar. A minute later, he disappeared around the back. As far as Molly knew, the only thing behind the hangar was a field. *What* could he be up to?

"Did you see the fellow leaving the hangar just now?" Molly dropped her voice low. "That was Dave, the mechanic I told you about. We'd better follow him and see what he's doing."

"What about Mr. Kay?" Anna asked. "Shouldn't we find him first? I want to know what the FBI agents said when he gave them the leaflet."

Molly fiddled with the rubber band on her braid, afraid to look into her friend's face.

"You found out something, didn't you?" Anna said suddenly, her tone slightly accusing. "Come on, Molly. *Tell me.*"

"Oh, Anna, the leaflet's still in Mr. Kay's coat pocket," Molly blurted.

When Anna didn't respond, Molly peeked up at her. Tears swam in her friend's eyes.

"Don't cry." Molly squeezed Anna's hand. "Maybe he just didn't get to it yesterday. I'll find him, and when I do, I'll ask him to *please* take the leaflet to the FBI. *Today.*"

Anna looked at Molly, her face filled with worry. Molly knew Anna was thinking of her brother sitting in jail—maybe even being sent off to an internment camp like the Kruegers.

"I *will* talk to Mr. Kay—I promise, Anna. But *Dave* is the Silver Shirt, and he was in such a hurry just now, he's *got* to be up to something." Tapping her chin, Molly gazed at the hangar. "Maybe he's got more leaflets stashed behind the hangar. If I don't check it out now, Anna, I may not have another chance."

"If *we*," Anna said with a sniffle.

"We?"

"*We* need to check it out."

Molly smiled at her friend. Anna gave a wobbly smile back, her cheeks tear-smudged.

"Maybe we'll find more proof that Dave's the real Silver Shirt. Then when Aunt Eleanor flies in this afternoon, we can tell her everything," Molly said, her excitement growing. "*She'll* convince the FBI that Max is innocent."

Anna wiped her eyes on her shirt sleeve. Then she looked at Molly and nodded firmly. "Let's get going."

Linking arms, the two girls ran across the grass toward the hangar.

They ran past the planes parked in front and hurried down the left side of the building. When they reached the back corner, they stopped. Cautiously, Molly peered around the corner. Junk parts, plane tires, and broken boards were piled along the rear wall of the hangar. The field, overgrown with tall grasses and weeds, stretched behind it. There was no sign of Dave.

Disappointment filled Molly one more time. "He's not back here. *Nothing's* back here."

"Where could he have gone?" Anna asked.

Molly looked at her friend, and a lump formed in her throat. "I'm sorry, Anna. If I'd been Jack or Doc from the A-1 Detective Agency, I would have made sure Mr. Kay took the leaflet to the FBI. And I wouldn't have lost Dave!"

"That's okay, Molly." Anna put her arm around Molly's shoulder and took a deep breath. "I know you're not a detective like Jack or Doc. But Molly, ever since Max was arrested, you've tried to help. You've been my best friend. To me, that's better than being an A-1 Detective."

Molly gave her friend a grateful smile, but Anna wasn't looking at Molly anymore. Her eyes were focused on something over Molly's shoulder.

"Hey, there's a shack way back in the field," Anna said. "Maybe Dave was going there."

Molly turned to look, shading her eyes against the sun. In the middle of the field, a rusty tin roof jutted above the weeds. A faint trail wound through the tall grasses and briars, stopping at the shack.

Molly studied the small building, which reminded her of Granpa's chicken coop. "What do you think could be in there?"

"I don't know. Maybe we should take a look," Anna said.

"But what if Dave's there?" Molly asked. "Running into him by the hangar was scary enough. I'd hate to bump into Dave in that deserted shack."

"If he is there, we'll spy on him long enough to find out what he's doing. Then we'll *run*."

Molly took a deep breath. "Okeydokey," she said breezily even though a shiver raced up her arms. As she made her way down the path after Anna, the brambles snagged her shorts and scratched her legs.

Ten feet from the shack, Anna stopped and put a finger to her lips. Molly craned her neck, trying to get a better look. The door of the shack was closed, and there was no sound but the faraway trill of a meadowlark.

Anna waved her ahead. When they reached the door, Molly could see that it was latched. Cobwebs hung like icicles from the sagging tin roof. Weeds and vines choked the slatted wood sides.

"It doesn't look as if anybody's here," Molly whispered, the scaredy-cat part of her glad that Dave *wasn't* there. "Actually, it looks like no one's used this place for ages."

"Then why aren't there any cobwebs around the door?" Anna asked.

Molly raised her brows. "Hey, you're right. And look, the latch on the door is shiny, not rusty, as if it's new. Somebody *has* been here recently." *As recently as today?* she wondered. *Had* Dave walked back here?

Molly gulped nervously. But then she realized that if the latch was hooked on the outside, no one could be inside. "I don't think he's in there now."

"Um, we'd better look inside?" Anna's statement ended in a question as if she wasn't too sure either.

"We should. Maybe Dave's storing leaflets or other kinds of contraband in there." Hesitantly, Molly reached for the latch, her fingers trembling. She lifted the lever, and slowly the door swung toward her, its hinges creaking.

Too scared to move, she stared into the dark interior. There were no windows, but light shining through the open door illuminated the back wall, which was lined with shelves. Rusty tins and mildewed boxes were stacked on the shelves. Old army-green footlockers sat on the dirt floor against both side walls.

Molly wrinkled her nose. "Pee-uw. This place smells like Granpa's cellar."

"Sure doesn't look like anyone's been in here," Anna said.

Molly stepped inside. A scrabbling noise around her feet made her jump back. She bumped into Anna, who let out a squeal.

"Just mice." Molly examined the foot-lockers. There were two of them. "There's a layer of dust on them an inch thick. I bet they've been stored in here forever. Wait, hold on." A gleam beside the doorway caught her attention. A third footlocker was stashed in the dark corner. She bent closer, noticing that its lid was clean. "This one looks as if it was just brought in here. Or someone wiped it off."

"Is it locked?" Anna asked.

"I'll check." Molly crouched beside it and felt for the metal latch. Anna watched over her shoulder. "It's *not* locked," Molly said. "Should I open it?"

"Jack and Doc would."

"Here goes, then. One, two, *three*." Molly pushed up the lid. Inside were two piles of neatly folded clothes. For a second, neither girl moved.

Then Anna snorted. "It's filled with *clothes?*"

Molly's shoulders slumped. "All this sneak-ing around for nothing."

"There *has* to be something more in there." Kneeling beside Molly, Anna pawed through the clothes. "Jeans. Jackets. Overalls. There *must* be something else!"

A flash of bright red under the overalls caught Molly's eye. She grasped the material and pulled it from the footlocker, shook out the folds, and held it up. It was a gray shirt. Across the front was a scarlet L.

Molly gasped. "A Silver Shirt!"

Gingerly, Anna touched the L. "Is this like the ones worn by the Silver Legion?"

"Yes!" Molly jumped up. "Anna, this is more proof against Dave!"

Creeeek. A noise rang out behind Molly. She spun around in time to see the door of the shack slam shut, plunging them into darkness.

"Wha— Hey!" Dropping the shirt, Molly lunged for the door. "Wait! Open the door. We're in here!"

She banged on the door and then stepped back, waiting for it to open. Instead, the latch clicked heavily into place.

Molly inhaled sharply. In the darkness, she felt Anna's fingers squeezing her shoulder.

"It sounds like someone's locking us in," Anna whispered hoarsely.

Molly jumped forward. "Don't lock this door. We're in here!" She pummeled the wooden door with her fists. Then together, she and Anna pushed on it with their shoulders. The door didn't budge.

Panic filled Molly. Blindly, she felt around for an inside knob or latch but found nothing. In the middle of the door, a sliver of sunlight shone through a crack between two boards. Quickly, Molly bent and put one eye to the crack. She could see a blur of movement and then the outline of an arm.

"Anna," Molly gasped. "Someone is right outside. And whoever it is must hear us yelling—which means he's locking us in *on purpose.*"

"On purpose!" Anna breathed. "Then it must be Dave. He must have followed us!"

Peering through the crack again, Molly

saw the figure move away from the door. As he stepped into the sunlight, Molly glimpsed a light blue shirt, *not* olive green coveralls. Then she spotted a gold emblem over the shirt pocket. She clapped a hand to her mouth, stifling a cry.

Not Dave. *Mr. Kay!*

10
TRAPPED

Molly watched as Mr. Kay turned and strode down the path toward the hangar. Then she lost sight of him. For a moment, she didn't say a word. She was too stunned. She'd *trusted* Mr. Kay.

Behind Molly, Anna moaned. "Dave must have seen us go into the shack. Oh, golly, we're done for now."

"It wasn't Dave." Molly's words were as heavy as her heart.

"Not Dave? Then *who?*"

"Mr. Kay."

"Mr. Kay?" Anna sounded confused.

Molly turned toward Anna. Her friend's face was pale in the dim light. "I saw him when he hurried off. *Mr. Kay* locked us in.

Maybe he's in cahoots with Dave."

Molly reached for Anna's hand, worried that Anna would dissolve into a puddle of tears.

Instead, Anna stepped around Molly and angrily kicked the door. "We've *got* to get out of here." *Kick.* "We've *got* to tell someone about Mr. Kay. We've *got* to save Max." *KICK.* Anna's last kick was so hard, her Camp Gowonagin cap flew off.

"Help! Help! Let us out!" Anna shouted. She pounded on the door. Molly joined her, figuring someone would surely hear.

The two girls hollered and banged until their voices were hoarse and their fists numb. Finally, Anna leaned her forehead against the door. "It's no use. All we've raised is dust and splinters."

"Let's rest awhile and try again." Molly tried to sound hopeful. "Someone might hear us when the airfield gets more crowded. Or maybe one of the mechanics will come around back. Or maybe our families will miss us and come looking."

Anna sighed. "Mama thinks I'm at your house."

"Grammy thinks I'm at your house."

"Even when they figure out we're missing, they'll never think of looking for us at the airfield." Anna heaved an even bigger sigh. "And as long as we're trapped way out here, we can't help Max."

"That must be why Mr. Kay didn't give the leaflet to the FBI," Molly decided. "He *wants* Max to look guilty."

Her gaze went to the gray shirt, lying atop the footlocker in the corner. "Anna, Mr. Kay must be a Silver Shirt. I'll bet *he's* the rat who put those leaflets in Aunt Eleanor's plane!"

Anna caught her breath. "I bet he saw us pull the Silver Shirt from the footlocker. I bet he locked us in so we couldn't show it to the FBI agents! Oh, Molly, we've got to do something. If Mr. Kay gets away, Max may *never* get out of jail."

"You're right," Molly agreed. "We've *got* to get out of here and tell someone." *What would the A-1 Detectives do?* "There's got to be another way out of here."

Anna tilted her head. "What about the roof?"

"We could try." The girls picked up two footlockers by the leather handles and stacked one on top of the other. Then Molly climbed on top. Anna stood behind her, holding her knees so that Molly wouldn't fall. Raising her arms high, she pushed on the roof.

"Ouch, it's hot." She snapped her hands away.

"I'll see if I can find something to push with," Anna said.

Molly blew on her fingertips, then tried again. The roof was nailed tightly.

"No good." She jumped down. Anna was poking through the boxes on the shelves that lined the back wall.

"Just old paint tins and brushes." She waved a paintbrush in front of Molly's face. "We could paint a hole in the wall and climb through it," she said solemnly. Then she burst into giggles, which turned into hiccups and then became sobs. "Let's f-f-f-face it. We're trapped. We'll never be able to help Max. He'll stay in jail or, even worse, he'll be sent far away to one of those camps. Maybe *forever*." Anna sank down on a footlocker and buried her face in her arms.

"Oh, Anna, don't give up." Molly picked the Camp Gowonagin cap off the ground, brushed it off, and gently put it on Anna's head.

Suddenly she heard voices outside. Then footsteps crunched in the dry weeds. Had Mr. Kay come back?

"Anna," she whispered. "Someone's coming."

The latch rattled. The two girls clung to each other. Molly sucked in her breath, her gaze riveted on the door. It had to be Mr. Kay— and he was trying to get in!

"Molly? Anna?"

"Aunt Eleanor!" Molly leaped to her feet and banged on the door. "We're in the shack. Let us out!"

She heard the latch lift and then the door

flew open. Sunlight poured in, and she and Anna flew into Aunt Eleanor's arms.

"We thought we'd be trapped in there forever!" Molly buried her face in the bib of her aunt's zoot suit. Aunt Eleanor hugged the girls tight, then shepherded them away from the doorway, out into the sunshine. From the corner of her eye, Molly saw a man in olive green coveralls go into the shack behind them.

"You scared me half to death!" Aunt Eleanor said. "What were you girls doing in that shack?"

"It's a long story," Molly replied, pulling back from her embrace. "But there's no time to waste." Just then, Molly noticed a man in a black suit standing behind her aunt. It was the tall FBI agent.

"Girls, this is Agent Danvers," Aunt Eleanor said.

"Gosh, I'm glad you're here!" Molly blurted. "Anna and I found proof that Mr. Kay, not Max, is the—" She was gesturing toward the shack, ready to explain about the Silver Shirt, when the man in the overalls stepped out. It was *Dave!*

He held out several yellow leaflets, a trimphant expression on his face. "See? They're propaganda leaflets like the ones found in Miss Culver's plane," he told Agent Danvers. "I found them in the footlocker in there. I told you Mr. Kay was up to no good."

"You mean *you* suspected Mr. Kay, too?" Molly asked him. *So Dave wasn't in cahoots with Mr. Kay?* "Is that why you were snooping back here this morning?"

"Dave was the one who led us to you," Aunt Eleanor said. "He saw you come back here, and then he saw Mr. Kay hurry from this direction as well. I flew in earlier than planned and Dave and Agent Danvers ran to meet me."

"Mr. Kay locked us in the shack!" Anna exclaimed angrily. "He wants Max to stay in jail!"

"Anna's right," Molly said. "*Mr. Kay* is the Silver Shirt, not Max." Ducking inside the shack, Molly found the gray shirt. She brought it out and held it up. "See? So come on, let's go find him." She started up the path.

Agent Danvers caught her arm. "Where'd you get that shirt?"

"In the *shack*." Molly's voice rose. Why wouldn't the agent believe her? Every second they wasted gave Mr. Kay another chance to get away.

"At first we thought it belonged to Dave," she added, casting an apologetic glance his way. "But now we know it belongs to Mr. Kay. Why *else* would he lock us in there?"

"The girls are right," Dave insisted. "The past several weeks, I've spotted Mr. Kay nosing around the planes on the airfield and in the hangar when he thought no one was looking. He's seemed awfully interested in every little nook and cranny of those planes. I'm sure he's the one who's been smuggling the leaflets."

"He was poking around the planes? That could explain the greasy fingerprints on the inside of the P-51's ammunition panel," Molly said. "That's more proof that he's the culprit!"

"You girls were snooping in my plane?" Aunt Eleanor asked. "Molly, I told you to leave the investigating to the grownups."

"Don't be too mad at them," Dave said. "They were braver than I was. Max is my friend. When he was arrested, I knew he was innocent. But I didn't say anything to the FBI agents because I had no proof that Mr. Kay was the guilty one. But when I found the leaflets in my lunch box, I knew Mr. Kay must have planted them there. I had to do something."

"Hold on." Agent Danvers waved one hand. "Why would Mr. Kay plant leaflets in your lunch box? We'd already arrested a suspect."

"I think Mr. Kay knew I was watching him," Dave explained. "I think he was warning me that if I tried to help Max, he could easily make *me* look guilty."

Molly flushed and bit her lip. "Um, it worked, too." Haltingly, she told the others about snooping in the lunch box and giving the leaflet to Mr. Kay. "He never intended to give it to you, Agent Danvers."

"I'm convinced," Aunt Eleanor declared. "Agent Danvers, I think there's more than enough proof that you arrested the wrong man."

"Which means you have to *hurry*," Molly urged. "Before Mr. Kay gets away."

Agent Danvers again held up one hand. "Not so fast. I agree, there's enough evidence for Agent Platt and me to *question* Mr. Kay," he said. "We still have to see whether there's enough proof to *arrest* him."

"I guess that will have to be good enough for now," Dave said. Turning, he started up the path.

Finally! Molly squeezed Anna's hand as they followed Dave and Agent Danvers. Her heart thumped. She hoped they weren't too late.

When they rounded the corner of the hangar, Molly looked toward the terminal. Mr. Kay was dashing down the steps, carrying a briefcase.

"There he is!" she cried. "And it looks like he's in a rush."

Dave broke into a run; Molly and Anna

were right behind him. Suddenly, Mr. Kay saw them coming. Fear filled his face. Frantically, he fumbled at his keys, unlocked the car door, and flung it open. Molly gasped. Was Mr. Kay going to get away?

"Oh no you don't, Kay!" Dave hollered. Sprinting across the parking lot, he reached the man as he was climbing into the car. Mr. Kay swung the briefcase, catching Dave across the cheek.

Dave staggered backward. The briefcase flew open and its contents scattered in the wind. Mixed in with the whirl of white papers, Molly spied flashes of yellow. Leaflets!

Molly dropped Anna's hand, and the two girls snatched at the papers as they blew past. Dave growled and lunged at Mr. Kay just as Agent Danvers and Aunt Eleanor reached the car.

"*Enough.* I'll take it from here," Agent Danvers ordered. When Dave backed off, the agent grasped Mr. Kay's upper arm. "Sir, you need to come with me for questioning."

"I will *not.* Let me go." Mr. Kay struggled

to free himself. "What is the meaning of this? I'm the *manager* of this airport! Have you all lost your minds?"

Stooping, Aunt Eleanor picked up a sheaf of papers that had fallen from the briefcase. Molly and Anna ran up, their hands filled with leaflets, just as Agent Platt hurried down the terminal steps. "What's going on?" he asked.

"*This* is what's going on," Aunt Eleanor replied. She held out the papers in her hand. "Flight plans—and propaganda leaflets. Mr. Kay had them in his briefcase. I'll bet he uses the flight plans to find out plane routes. That way he knows when and where to hide his propaganda."

Agent Danvers pulled handcuffs from his back pocket and snapped them onto Mr. Kay's wrists. "Agent Platt, collect the briefcase and other evidence, please," he added as he steered Mr. Kay toward the black FBI car.

Side by side, Molly and Anna watched as Agent Danvers put Mr. Kay into the backseat.

When the door slammed shut, Molly breathed a sigh of satisfaction. Beside her, Anna beamed happily.

"Whew." Dave wiped his brow. "That was a close one. I thought Mr. Kay was going to get away."

"Thanks to you, he didn't." Aunt Eleanor gently touched his scraped cheek. "You're going to have a nasty bruise."

"That's nothing compared to what Molly and Anna went through." Dave turned to the girls. "Neither of you ever gave up on helping Max."

"We knew Max was innocent," Molly said. "And now the whole town will know who's the *real* Silver Shirt."

Anna nodded in agreement. "Agent Danvers and Agent Platt will put Mr. Kay in jail and let Max go!"

Leaning down, Aunt Eleanor gave them both a hug. "I'm glad we found you safe and sound. You were both so brave." She frowned with fake fierceness. "Even if you *did* disobey."

Molly winced, but then Eleanor's frown changed to a smile, and Molly and Anna laughed with relief.

"We *were* brave, weren't we, Anna?" Molly squeezed her friend's hand.

"Just as brave as the A-1 Detectives," Anna said firmly. Then with a whoop of joy, she tossed the Camp Gowonagin cap in the air. "And now Max will be coming home!"

11
A LETTER FOR MOLLY

"Molly, wake up."

"Hmmm?" Molly cracked open one eye. Aunt Eleanor sat on the edge of her bed. She held out a cup of water. Molly struggled up on one elbow. "What time is it?" she mumbled, her tongue thick.

"It's Sunday morning. You slept like a log all night. Here, drink this. You're still parched from yesterday's adventure."

"Yuck. I am." She took several sips. "Any news about Max? Is he home yet?"

"No news yet. We'll keep our fingers crossed, shall we?" She patted Molly's knee under the sheet. "I got permission to stick around until Monday so that I can see my sister and all the little McIntires. They should arrive this noon, in time for Sunday dinner."

"Your sister?" Molly repeated. Then she let out an "ohhhhh" of understanding. "You mean my mother. In all the excitement, I'd forgotten they were coming today. Gee, I'd better hurry. I can't go home without talking to Anna. I need to say good-bye and find out about Max and . . ."

With a laugh, Aunt Eleanor stood up. "Then get out of bed, sleepyhead."

Molly pulled on shorts and a shirt and ran downstairs.

Grammy set a bowl of oatmeal on the table. "I see you spent hours combing your hair," she teased.

Molly inspected a braid. Hairs stuck out every which way. "No time. Gotta say good-bye to Anna."

Molly was about to rush out the door when Grammy put a hand on her arm.

"You'll be back soon?" she asked.

"Promise. I'll bike straight to the Schulzes' and straight back."

"Please do. Yesterday almost did me in."
Grammy placed her palm over her heart. "And
don't stay long. You still need to pack and..."
She began to list all the things Molly needed
to do to prepare for her trip home.

Molly bounced from foot to foot. She wanted
to get to Anna's. Maybe the Schulzes would
even give her hugs of thanks. She puffed out
her chest, feeling a little proud. Even Granpa
had been secretly proud of her and Anna, at
least enough not to be *too* mad.

Grammy's chuckle interrupted Molly's
thoughts. "I can see you're not even listening.
So scoot, young lady." She flapped her apron,
shooing Molly out the kitchen door.

Granpa had propped her bike against the
porch railing. Grabbing the handlebars, Molly
pushed it from the yard. She ran alongside,
leaped onto the seat, and pumped furiously
down the lane.

As Molly pedaled, an ache filled her.
Tomorrow she'd be back home in Jefferson.
This would be the last time she'd ride over

to Anna's—the last time she'd see her friend this summer.

I'll really miss her!

As soon as she got back to Jefferson, she'd visit her friends Susan and Linda and tell them all about her adventure. They'd be astounded, and envious that they hadn't been involved. Then next week, school would start, and her days would be filled with lessons and homework. In all the hustle and bustle, would she forget this past week?

I'll never forget, Molly knew. *I'll remember this week for the rest of my life.*

Molly turned down the Schulzes' lane, picturing the day when the black car had zoomed past with the FBI agents. She coasted past the cornstalks, her braids flying.

When she caught sight of the Schulzes' house, she stood up, leaned over the handlebars, and pedaled hard the last hundred yards.

"Anna," Molly called, hoping her friend would come running from the house to meet

her. Braking sharply in front of the porch, she
jumped off the bike and put down the kick-
stand. "Anna!"

Molly bounded up the porch steps and
tried the front door. It was closed and locked.
Had all of them gone to town to pick up
Max?

Then she noticed that the front windows
were shuttered, which was odd on a hot
summer day. She tried to peer between the
shutters, but they were latched tight. Turning,
she went down the steps, the soles of her
Keds thudding so loudly they echoed.

A feeling of unease crept over Molly. She
ran around the house to the side window.
Standing on tiptoe, she was able to see into
the Schulzes' living room. Her eyes widened.
The furniture was draped with sheets.

What is going on? Molly wondered as she
raced around the house to the back porch.
She tried the back door, but it was also shut
and locked. Then she rapped on the window
and called again, "Anna?" Cupping her hands

around her face, she peered through the glass into the kitchen. Several cupboard doors hung open, and the shelves were bare.

Molly jerked back from the window. It looked as if the Schulzes had left!

But why? And where? And for how long?

And why didn't they say good-bye? Tears of disappointment sprang into Molly's eyes. Just a few minutes ago, she'd been so excited to see Anna again. So excited to hear good news about Max.

Blinking back tears, Molly ran across the backyard to the barn. The big doors were shut. "Anna?" she called, softly this time, as if she knew no one would answer.

A shiver ran up Molly's arms. She rubbed them, feeling chilled.

The farm was empty. It was as if the whole family had disappeared.

Suddenly, Molly's stomach twisted. What if all her and Anna's detective work hadn't helped the Schulzes at all? What if the FBI had taken them away to an internment camp, just like their friends the Kruegers?

No. No, that couldn't happen, Molly told herself as she walked slowly back to her bike.

But as she pedaled up the Schulzes' lane, a feeling of dread filled her.

★

An hour later, Molly laid her plaid shorts on top of the pile of clothes in her suitcase. Twisting one braid, she glanced around the bedroom, checking to make sure she'd packed everything. Any minute her mother, sister, and brothers would be here.

Seeing them will be so . . . Molly's thoughts trailed off and she plopped onto the bed, suddenly not caring.

Oh, Anna, where are you?

After Molly had biked home from the Schulzes', she'd told everyone that the family had left. Immediately, Granpa and Aunt Eleanor had driven to Weston to find out if anyone knew where they had gone.

Molly bit at her fingernail. She kept picturing Anna living in a tent surrounded by barbed wire, and the thought made her shudder.

Suddenly, footsteps thudded up the wooden stairs. Molly jumped up from the bed just as Aunt Eleanor came into the room.

"What did you find out?"

Aunt Eleanor shook her head. "Nothing, except…" She held out a letter. "Granpa picked this up at the general store," she said quietly. "Mr. Ringer said that someone had slipped it under the door. It has your name on it."

Wide-eyed, Molly glanced from the letter to Aunt Eleanor's face. Her aunt's lips were pressed in a tight line. Instantly, Molly knew that the letter was from Anna.

Aunt Eleanor handed her the envelope. There was no return address. Molly sank down on the bed and carefully tore the envelope open and read:

A Letter for Molly

To my dear friend Molly,

I'm sorry I didn't get to say good-bye to you.

Max came home last night. We were so excited! But then the FBI agents came back, too. They ransacked the house again. They said they still suspected that Papa and Max were aiding the Germans.

Oh, Molly, I was so scared. Then I thought of how brave you were. I told the agents that Mr. Kay was the Silver Shirt, not Max and Papa.

The FBI agents left. But they warned us that they would return. Papa said that he and Max were not safe anymore in Weston. Papa said they needed to leave. Mama said that we would all go. We packed quickly. We closed up the house. We are driving far away to stay with friends.

I am giving you the address of where we are going. Keep it a secret!

I will understand if you do not write to me. America is at war, and the FBI

thinks my family is the enemy. I hope,
dear Molly, that you will still think of me
as a friend.

Love,
Anna Schulz

P.S. I will wear your Camp Gowonagin cap
every day.

Molly finished reading the letter, tears blurring the words. No wonder Anna hadn't said good-bye!

"May I read it?" Aunt Eleanor asked softly.

Molly nodded. When Aunt Eleanor finished reading, she exhaled deeply. "I'm glad they're together and safe."

"Me, too," Molly said. "I thought the FBI had taken them to an internment camp, like their friends the Kruegers!"

Eleanor sat down beside Molly and took her hand. "I'm glad as well that they aren't in a camp. But Molly, you must realize that it may be a long time before you see Anna again. Mr. Schulz also left a note for Granpa, asking him to sell the chickens and cows."

"But why'd they have to leave?" Molly asked. Aunt Eleanor handed the letter back to Molly, and she stared blindly down at it. "Anna and her family didn't do anything wrong."

"Things change during wartime, Molly. To keep America safe, the government sometimes puts security first."

"So the Schulzes had to leave because they're *German*," Molly said bitterly.

"Yes."

"Well, that's unfair!" Molly jumped up, the letter clutched in her fingers. "Anna and I proved that Mr. Kay was smuggling those leaflets, not Max."

"I know. And your granpa and I are going to do everything we can to convince the FBI that the Schulzes *didn't* do anything wrong."

"But what can *I* do?" Molly felt helpless.

Turning sideways, Aunt Eleanor pulled out the top drawer of the bedside table. She rooted around for a moment and then handed

Molly a sheet of stationery and a pencil. "Sit down and write to Anna. That's what you can do."

"It's not much," Molly muttered.

Aunt Eleanor smiled. "Think how important your father's letters are to you," she reminded Molly as she stood up. "Now, I've got to pack too. I fly out early tomorrow morning."

After her aunt had left, Molly slumped on the mattress beside the bedside table. Shoulders hunched, chin propped in her palm, she tried to think what to write.

She thought about her father working far away in England, the Schulzes driving far away to a safe place, and her Aunt Eleanor flying far away in her P-51.

War had changed *everything*. Wartime in America wasn't just about collecting cans, rationing, and Victory gardens, Molly realized. It was about friends and family *never* being the same again.

Picking up the pencil, Molly began her letter:

A LETTER FOR MOLLY

Dear Anna,

I am so sorry I didn't get to say good-bye to you, too. My aunt tried to explain why the FBI agents still suspect your family. I don't understand it all, but I do know that I will always be your friend.

Try not to be too scared while you are away. As soon as this war is over, you will come home! And try not to be too homesick for your farm. When I was homesick at Camp Gowonagin, my mother would send me a hug in a letter. So look carefully inside this envelope because there is a hug for you.

Love,

Molly McIntire

P.S. Please write back.

P.P.S. Your secret is safe with me.

P.P.P.S. Every time you wear my cap, think of me. I'll be thinking of you, my forever friend!

GLOSSARY OF GERMAN WORDS

NOTE: *In German spelling, the letters "ch" stand for a sound similar to a very strong "h." (Think of the last sound in the name of the German composer, Bach.) In the pronunciations below, this sound is shown by the symbol ᶜH.*

ach (*ahᶜH*)—an expression similar to "oh" or "oh, dear"

Frau (*frow, rhymes with "how"*)—wife

Kinder (*KIN-der*)—children

mein (*mine*)—my

Schulz (*shooltz, with the "oo" pronounced as in "took"*)— a common German last name

Sohn (*zone*)—son

Tochter (*TAHᶜH-ter*)—daughter

und (*oont, with the "oo" pronounced as in "too"*)—and

OURS...to fight for

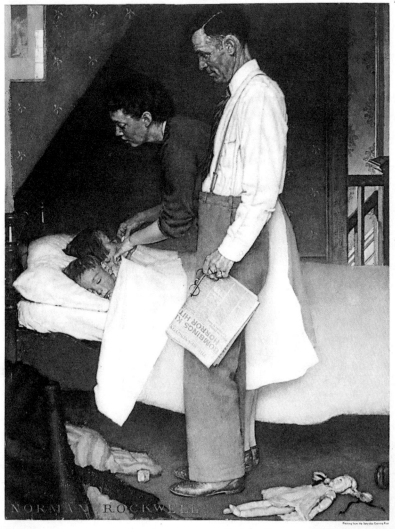

FREEDOM FROM FEAR

LOOKING BACK

A PEEK INTO THE PAST

This girl pauses in her chores to listen to the war news on the radio. Her father was a soldier.

For girls growing up in the 1940s, the war was never far from their minds. They worried about relatives who were serving overseas, just as Molly worried about her father. Sometimes they wondered if the fighting would ever end. Still, in their day-to-day lives they felt safe. The fighting was far away—all the way across the Atlantic Ocean in Europe and across the Pacific in Japan. At home in the United States, daily life went on pretty normally for most Americans.

For some families, however, life changed

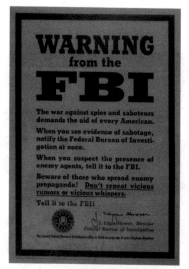

THE MILWAUKEE JOURNAL

Three Japanese Warships Sunk;
U.S. at War With Germany, Italy

Four Wake Island
Attacks Beaten Off

dramatically when America entered the war after Japanese planes bombed Pearl Harbor on December 7, 1941. Because Germany, Italy, and Japan were now enemies of the U.S., Americans who had come from those countries suddenly fell under suspicion. The Federal Bureau of Investigation, or FBI, started investigating anyone who might possibly be a traitor or spy. Many people were investigated simply because they had been born in an enemy country—even though, like the Schulzes, most of them had lived in America for decades and were completely loyal to the United States.

It didn't take much for the FBI to decide that people of German citizenship—or *enemy aliens*, as the government called them—

WARNING
from the
FBI

The war against spies and saboteurs demands the aid of every American.

When you see evidence of sabotage, notify the Federal Bureau of Investigation at once.

When you suspect the presence of enemy agents, tell it to the FBI.

Beware of those who spread enemy propaganda! **Don't repeat vicious rumors or vicious whispers.**

Tell it to the FBI!

J. Edgar Hoover, Director
Federal Bureau of Investigation

posed a risk to U.S. security. For example, a person who had sent money to relatives back in Germany or who had expressed sympathy for Germany's situation, even long ago before the war, was likely to be arrested. One seventeen-year-old boy about the same age as Anna's brother Max was arrested by FBI agents. In jail, they questioned him about community picnics he had attended at his town's German-American Day celebration!

When a man was arrested, his wife and children often didn't learn for weeks where he was being held, or why. Sometimes both parents were put in jail, and their children were placed in orphanages or left to fend for themselves if they were

NOTICE TO ALIENS OF ENEMY NATIONALITIES

* The United States Government requires all aliens of German, Italian, or Japanese nationality to apply at post offices nearest to their place of residence for a Certificate of Identification. Applications must be filed between the period February 9 through February 28, 1942. Go to your postmaster today for printed directions.

Japanese Americans being taken away. As the train leaves, this family shows its patriotism and hope for peace.

old enough. After being investigated by the FBI, thousands of German and Japanese families were sent away to internment camps, where they were confined for years. The Schulzes knew this had happened to their friends the Kreugers and were afraid it would happen to them.

German American teenager Amelia Kesselring was interned with her parents.

Life in an internment camp was a bit better than being in prison, because the children could attend school and families were able to stay together, but their lives were never the same again. Interned families lost their homes and farms, their jobs, their dignity, and their freedom from fear. Although they were treated like criminals, almost none of them were found to be spies or traitors.

Some German Americans were interned at this camp in Tennessee.

In fact, *Nazi sympathizers*, or people who shared Hitler's beliefs, tended to be ordinary Americans like Mr. Kay. Most Americans hated Hitler and believed he was a dangerous enemy. But his ideas did appeal to some Americans who wanted the U.S. to get rid of anyone who was not white and Christian, as Germany was doing. One

Nazi leader Adolf Hitler wanted Germany to be racially "pure." He condemned millions of innocent people to death.

Hitler supporter, William Dudley Pelley, founded the Silver Legion of America, an organization that published pro-Nazi propaganda and attracted 15,000 members.

When the U.S. entered the war, President Roosevelt told the FBI to arrest Pelley. He was

imprisoned for *sedition*, or urging actions against the United States. Despite Pelley's imprisonment,

A rare photo of a Silver Shirts meeting

the Silver Shirts continued to spread propaganda any way they could. One way was to hide propaganda leaflets in airplanes, as Molly discovered!

Airplanes served important roles in World War Two. They were used to

The powerful P-51 fighter plane

drop bombs over enemy territory in Europe and Japan and to move military personnel and supplies around the U.S. With all the military pilots dedicated to missions overseas, there weren't enough pilots on the home front to test-fly new models and *ferry*, or deliver, new planes from factories to military bases. So the Women's Airforce Service Pilot, or WASP, program was formed to fill those roles.

In Molly's time, very few women knew how

to fly planes, but many wanted to learn. More than 25,000

WASPs in training

women applied to become WASPs, but requirements were strict and only 1,830 were accepted. They spent six months training in the small town of Sweetwater, Texas. Just as Molly admired Aunt Eleanor, the girls growing up in Sweetwater greatly admired the WASPs. When they saw one around town, the girls would point and tell each other, "She can fly those big airplanes!"

As a WASP, Aunt Eleanor would have been an expert pilot. Although the WASPs were not allowed to fly in combat, they did face real risks. One of their most dangerous jobs was towing an airborne target for a male pilot-in-training to

practice shooting at from another plane. In the two years of the WASP program, 35 WASPs lost their lives while

WASPs proudly wore these silver wings on their uniforms.

flying. But to these bold young women, the risk was worth it. "I don't know of a WASP that didn't really truly love flying," said one WASP 50 years later. "The ability to do something you love and to do it at a time of need for your country—nothing is better than that."

Today, women can be military pilots. Below are the first women to graduate from the U.S. Air Force Academy, in 1977.

About the Author

Alison Hart has written more than twenty books for children and young adults, including *Danger at the Wild West Show* in the American Girl History Mysteries series. Her book *Shadow Horse* was nominated for the 2000 Edgar Allan Poe Award for Best Children's Mystery.

Ms. Hart teaches English and creative writing at Blue Ridge Community College in Virginia and is a court-appointed special advocate for abused and neglected children. Pursuing her longtime interest in mysteries and crime investigation, Ms. Hart is also a graduate of the Staunton Citizens Police Academy.

She lives in Virginia with her husband, two kids, three horses, two dogs, and a guinea pig.